THE SECRET CHILD

a novel by MARTI HEALY

ISBN 978-0-9791277-7-9

First Edition

Design by Barry Doss.
Cover illustration by Pam Verenes.
Celtic symbols by Cathey Henley Osborne.

Printed in China.

The Design Group Press, LLC
832 Brandy Road
Aiken, South Carolina 29801

DEDICATED TO

B.L.D.

Cian, the ancient one, looked upon the spirit that was crouched and shimmering before him. The moon slid peacefully across the Bay and came to rest under his outstretched feet. He sat absolutely still and listened fondly to the voices of the forest that whispered and sang all around him.

"Tell me the dream," he said at last to the spirit.

"The dream is of a new daughter among us," she replied. "She is surrounded in secrets, unseen by most; a mystical one in her own right."

Cian nodded and smiled and sighed into the wind, "Yes. I, too, have seen the vision. A secret child is coming."

Spring
1855

The Arrival.

Marika stood motionless in the deeply shadowed corner of the train's last passenger car as it waited puffing and groaning impatiently in the station. To her right was the open door. A window lowered to half height was to her left. A great puff of steam heaved itself into the car interior on the strong spring breeze and concealed Marika's presence even more thoroughly.

Across the aisle from her, now partially hidden from her own eyes, was a gathering of strangers. Kind people, she sensed; genuinely concerned for the welfare of the young boy who lay sick and silent and alone on the first seat facing them.

"Doesn't *anyone* know who he is?" one of the men asked incredulously. The speaker appeared to be the town's doctor. He had come aboard just a few minutes earlier following a woman who had gone with haste to fetch him. He had quickly felt the boy's fever and weak pulse.

"No one seems to have noticed him," the train conductor at the doctor's side replied. "Of course, I did when we stopped," he continued half apologetically. "And I could see right off he was ailing bad. But there weren't nobody with him. Nobody that knew his name or even where he got onto the train."

Marika considered the compelling possibility of stepping

forward. But what would she say? Perhaps she could tell them that he's her brother and that his name is Daniel and he's five years old. Perhaps she could reveal that they boarded the train in Boston. What she wanted most was to simply plead with them to help him. But every day of her short thirteen-year-old life had been spent learning to keep her silence. Especially when among the "others." Especially when you were in the others' world, away from your own people.

"Please, please help him," she shouted out in her mind, her eyes shut tightly in concentration and against burning tears. "He's so sick. I love him more than my life. Please!"

As often happened when Marika cast her thoughts strongly focused toward others, people acted on them without really knowing why.

"We must help him, of course," the doctor said suddenly, and he carefully slid his arms under the boy's slight body. He lifted the child with tenderness, noting that the home-woven blanket weighed almost as much as the small human body within it.

"Where are you going to take him?" asked the conductor. "I've got to tell the company – got to make a report."

The doctor called over his shoulder, "I'll take him to the widow Nydegger's place. You see if you can find a ticket or something that will tell us who he is and where he came from – or where he was *going*!" Under his breath he continued his remarks as he stepped off the train and hurried through the station, "How can *any* parents put a small child on a train all alone, with no note, no identification ... and a sick child at that!" His fear for the boy outraged him against an unknown family. He had quickly looked over the child's clothing and found them not very clean and mended many times. But there was no way of telling their origin. No ticket was tucked in a pocket or pinned to his jacket. No one to watch over him! Anger drove his feet faster.

While the conductor was watching the doctor disembark down the steep steps of the train on the side that faced the town, Marika slipped out of the corner shadows and retrieved two worn carpetbags, which had been shoved deeply beneath the bench seat where the boy had lain. Some of the passengers had gotten off the train at this station and waited out of compassionate curiosity, watching until the doctor departed. Those who remained on the train were craning to see the hurried doctor and his bundle out the windows, and clucking their tongues in genuine pity but also with a bit of embarrassed relief that the feverish child that no one had noticed was now out of their midst.

On the opposite side of the train, Marika simply tossed the bags to the ground and scaled down the ladder-like steps. She quickly skirted around the back end of the car, and walked with purpose and lowered head, a bag in either hand, in the direction the doctor had taken her brother. No one seemed to see her cautiously trailing behind him.

By the time the conductor turned back to search the area where the boy had been found alone, there was nothing to identify the child and no trace of an older sister. Only a small tin cup filled with water was abandoned on the floor in the corner nearest the door. It was still cool from the oak rain barrel behind the station where Marika had dipped it. Wet rings remained, darkening the scuffed wooden floor beneath it. The conductor picked it up and noted the fine craftsmanship of the small vessel. Then he emptied it out of the open window and absently slipped it into his coat's side pocket.

It had been upon returning from her quest to fill her cup that Marika had found the people surrounding Danny. She realized no one suspected that she – or anyone – had been with him, nor that this very station in the midlands of South Carolina had been their intended destination.

When Doctor Walter Jackson reached the other side of the railway platform, he went directly to a waiting horse-drawn buggy. It was a small black carriage with a single bench seat across the front and two large spoked wheels on either side. A calm chestnut mare was hitched to it, watching with alert intelligence as the doctor approached. A middle-aged black man was standing at her head, her reins in his hand.

As if the child in his arms were completely weightless, the doctor shifted him to his left arm and shoulder, and handed his bag to the waiting black man. The man took the bag and tucked it neatly under the seat with practiced ease. He then cupped his right hand under the doctor's elbow to steady him as the doctor swung himself and his bundle into the seat, and then handed the doctor the reins with his left hand. The two worked together with fluidity, a team long used to each other's movements.

"Joseph," the doctor spoke to the man, "run to Miss Nydegger's house and tell her I'm coming with a very ill child."

The man started on his way as the doctor was finishing his sentence.

"Joseph," the doctor called out again. The running man quickly turned to face the doctor but continued to jog in place. "Tell her ... tell her ..." the doctor looked down at the child cradled in his arm, the tiny face so pale his veins looked dark against his temples, his damp hair matted against his head.

"Never mind, Joseph, just tell her I'll be there as fast as I can."

"Yessir," Joseph replied. He understood well enough the urgency in the doctor's voice and shoulders. He could read that man's face like his own heart. That child was very ill, indeed. Like-as-not, he wasn't going to make it through the night.

Just as Joseph turned to his task, he thought he glimpsed a shadow behind the doctor's carriage – perhaps another child. But he couldn't be sure. And he couldn't stay to find out.

Joseph ran through the streets and cut through alleys and behind stores with an athletic grace that belied his age. The people of the town who saw him knew he would be on an errand for Doc Jackson, and that someone must be sick. Joseph could angle and jog his way through yards and fences and back gates and fields quicker than anyone – certainly faster than a horse and carriage could make its way along the dirt streets and rutted roads of the town.

Marika followed as closely as she could to the buggy that carried her beloved brother. She struggled with the baggage, meager as it was, but her concern for Daniel kept her feet moving at pace with the buggy and its passengers.

Just on the edge of the other side of town, the carriage pulled up to the front of a neat and attractive stone and wood house. It was compact and obviously very well built. To the west side of the house was a barn; a grassy, shaded horse paddock joined the two. Behind the house was a large garden; the strawberry plants and mint and damp dirt all rode the late afternoon breezes with tempting fragrance. A black and brown shaggy-haired dog came trotting around the side of the house at the sound of the buggy's arrival.

"Whoa there, Molly," the doctor reined in the horse. "Hey, Scout," he spoke absently to the dog. But the dog was looking beyond him, farther down the lane in the direction from which the buggy had come. Doc quickly looped the reins around the lip of the whip holder at the edge of the buggy, and stepped carefully down from the seat, hugging the small boy to his left shoulder, listening for signs of consciousness, hearing only his shallow breathing.

"Wait here, girl," he spoke quietly to the horse. But at that moment, Joseph came out through the open front door of the cottage and went immediately to the horse and buggy. He pulled the medical bag from under the seat and handed it to Doc Jackson, and then moved toward the mare's head.

"Thanks, Joseph. Everything all right?" the doctor inquired.

"Yessir. Miss Nydegger's inside getting a cot ready in the room off the kitchen."

Doc Jackson stepped up the large, smooth stones leading to the porch and ducked through the low wooden front door without knocking.

"Magdalena," he called. "Maggie, it's me, Walt Jackson."

"Back here," a woman's voice answered from the rear of the house. "Bring him on through."

The floors creaked under the weight of the doctor's quick step as he passed first through a well-proportioned living room filled with comfortable seating, a small square piano, and a white-clothed table; ladder back chairs hung from pegs on one wall. He walked with familiarity through a painted swinging door into a large, windowed kitchen, and finally on into a small cozy room on the backside of the kitchen's massive fireplace.

Outside, in front of the house, Joseph looked down to speak to Scout, the dog, but a flit of color caught the corner of his eye. He raised his head quickly, but could see nothing and no one. In the same moment, Scout was disappearing around the side of the house.

Marika placed her open hand gently on the muzzle of the dog as she slid past the corner of the house, peeking in the windows on tiptoe as she went. A room filled with chairs and a table. A kitchen with its windows open, so she could hear the doctor's steps and his voice as he spoke to a woman just out of sight. The next window at the very back of the house revealed a small cot placed near the brick backside of a fireplace. It would be warm and comforting for her brother. Fresh white sheets and a soft pillow and a thick, down-filled quilt awaited him, too. The woman was just smoothing the top of them as the doctor entered the room. Marika's stomach eased slightly as she saw the preparations lovingly being made for Daniel. Scout cocked his head at her silently, questioningly. She shook her head from side to side slowly, looking him full in the eyes, and the dog trotted away.

Around the next corner of the house, a large wooden porch jutted out under a slanted roof. The floor of the porch was raised a good two feet from the ground for air circulation, and Marika shoved her two carpetbags quickly under one edge. She pushed them hard across the dirt until they were safely out of sight.

The voices from inside were muffled through the closed windows, and they spoke in hushed tones. Marika shut her eyes in concentrated listening.

"Lay him down here, Doc. Let's get him into something clean. Here's a shirt we can dress him in."

"I'll get some water."

"There's some warming in a pot on the stove. It should be just about ready now. There's also some cool water fresh from the well waiting in a pot in the sink. Clean towels are on the table."

Sounds of movement filtered through to Marika, and she took the chance of raising herself to look into the window again.

The woman bending and fussing over Daniel was about fifty, Marika guessed – near the age of her own grandmother. But this woman was of a more stocky build; softer, rounder. Gran had been all skin and bones; hard angles carved out of a hard life.

Marika's heart gave a sudden leap at the memory of her grandmother. Her absence from Marika's life left great, jagged edges. Gran would have taken care of Danny's illness. Mixtures, wraps, cloths soaked in herbs and grasses, strong-smelling poultices.

Gran wouldn't have let Danny become so ill, Marika believed with her whole heart. And Gran would never have let him be taken by "others."

"I'm sorry, Danny," Marika whispered under the breeze. "I'm so very sorry. I love you so."

Then she slipped into her Irish, as she willed her thoughts into Danny: *"Tá grá agam duit. Tá bóm órm."* (I love you. I'm sorry.)

Danny moaned softly.

"Doc?" the woman said with hope.

The doctor felt the boy's pulse and put his large hand against the tiny cheek. "I'm afraid not, Maggie. 'Fraid it's just the fever talking through him."

"Can't you give him something?"

"Not when he's this sick. He can't swallow anything. He can't even take water. All we can do is try to keep him comfortable. Keep bathing his face in cool water. . .keep his lips moistened. Maybe the fever will run its course."

"But you don't think it will, do you," she said, her voice catching.

The doctor didn't respond. Marika did, with a sudden sob.

The doctor went to the window and looked out as the sun was starting to set. "Did you hear something?" he said to the woman over his shoulder.

"No. The wind, perhaps. Perhaps the angels waiting nearby for this little one's soul."

"Yes."

Doc looked down at Scout, who had come quietly into the room to sniff over the sick boy. The faithful animal lay at the cot's side with vigilance, but showed no sign of anything warranting concern outside the house.

With her back pressed flat against the outside wall under the window, Marika wept silent tears and prayed with open arms

16

reaching to heaven. "Please, God, don't take him, not Daniel, not Daniel, not Danny. Please."

With all her innocent faith she prayed, with all the sincerity of youth: "Please take me instead, please take me, please not Danny, please."

Again, Marika slipped into a comforting tongue and began to pray in Shelta, the secret language of the Irish "Travellers," the gypsies, the words of her own people:

Mwilsha's gater, swart a manyath,
   (Our Father, who is in heaven,)
Manyi graw a kradji dilsha's manik.
   (Hallowed be your name.)
Graw bi greydid, sheydi laadu
   (Your kingdom come, your will be done,)
Az aswart in manyath.
   (On earth as it is in heaven.)
Bag mwilsha talosk minyart goshta dura.
   (Give us today our daily bread.)
Geychel aur shaaku areyk mwilsha
   (And forgive us our sins,)
Geychas needjas greydi gyamyath mwilsha.
   (As we forgive those who sin against us.)
Nijesh solk mwil start gyamyath,
   (Save us from the time of trial,)
Bat bog mwilsha ahim gyamyath.
   (And deliver us from evil.)
Diyil the sridag, taajirath an manyath
   (For the kingdom, the power, and the glory are yours,)
Gradum a gradum.
   (Now and forever.)

Danny moved his head. His eyes fluttered, but remained shut. His lips moved slightly, following the words his sister was praying just a few feet away.

"Hush, Baby," the woman answered him. "It's all right. I'm here, I'm here," she crooned to him.

Scout sighed deeply.

A knock at the door to the room caused both adults to turn and face Joseph as he stood in the open doorway. "People are here," he said. "People from town have heard about the little boy. Want to know if there is anything they can do. Want to know how he's doing."

"Thank you, Joseph. Please tell them thank you, but Miss Nydegger is doing all that can be done right now."

"Ask them to pray," Maggie said to Joseph. "That never can hurt."

"Yes'm," Joseph answered. His eyes went to the doctor's face. The doctor shook his head. "Yes'm," Joseph repeated. "I'll pray with them, too."

Scout joined Joseph as he returned to the front steps of the house and paused before the group of people who had gathered there in the twilight. They stood in small groups of twos and threes. They spoke in hushed, sad comments. A few children were among them.

"I'm afraid Doc Jackson may not be able to save this one," Joseph said quietly. The people were silent. "Miss Maggie calls us to pray," his voice was just above a whisper. Then he walked over to the edge of the porch and sat down, his legs hanging over the side. Others took his cue and began to sit, to pray, to wait. Scout took his place near Joseph's left hand.

Joseph began to hum a Spiritual nearly under his breath as he stroked the dog's neck. He hummed in deep baritone and looked around the side of the house. Nothing was in sight in the darkening

18

shadows. But he thought he might have heard the cry of a bird. He thought his humming might cover the sound, because he knew, somehow, it wanted to be covered.

The little boy died in silence and peace just at midnight. Both Maggie and Scout were at his side.

The people took their children and each other home and spread the word to the rest of the town. Maggie prepared his small body for burial. Doc Jackson and Joseph got a child's casket from the undertaker and brought it over to Maggie's house.

The night before, when Maggie had been changing the boy from his dirt-worn clothing into a large clean shirt, she had discovered a very small St. Christopher medal fashioned out of silver on a chain tucked into the toe of his left shoe. She was a strong Quaker herself, but she surmised that he may have been Catholic and respected that possibility. She sent one of her neighbors to ask the local priest to perform the burial ceremony.

By mid-morning, when the procession started to the cemetery, there were at least fifty people in front of the house. Doc and Joseph carried the casket between them on their shoulders. Joseph remarked at the lightness of it. Doc kept touching it with his hand, reassuring himself that it was still there.

Someone had brought a fife, another a drum, and yet another a small accordion, and quiet music began to pace their steps to the graveyard. It was just to the north of town, and people joined the walk as they proceeded. Some in silence. Some singing the familiar words to the hymns being played. Now, there were nearly a hundred.

Reaching the edge of the cemetery, the music turned to "Nearer My God to Thee," and most all began to sing then. It seemed to

Maggie that almost everyone in town must have been there.

The cemetery was compellingly beautiful, about five decades old. It was laid out with family plots and areas devoted to soldiers and specially edged graves that cradled children. Some of the more moneyed families had remembered their lost with large monuments of marble and granite deeply carved with scripture and poetry. Sculptures and statues of great symbolism offered lasting messages of loving tribute – guardian angels and resting lambs and urns draped in mourning.

There were great oak trees and cypress along the pathways, creating welcoming shade. Their branches arched protectively across the departed and mourners alike, and caught the sighs of breezes that spoke of God being near.

Close to the place where the little boy would be buried, a summer house – a white-painted gazebo – had been built. Families would come here on hot Sunday afternoons. And birds would nest in its eaves. And Danny would not be alone.

The sun sparkled of promise and wisps of white clouds made the sky look like it had been swept with angel wings.

The priest said kind words and gentle prayers. He performed the ceremony with love and respect for this unknown, unnamed child. They laid him to rest, and people took handsful of dirt in turn to drop into the small grave, then laid at its edges the flowers they had brought from their gardens and fields.

Everyone prayed and cried and then turned to leave, processing together as they had arrived. The singing had ceased, but the musicians played again until only the lightest of notes floated back on the afternoon breeze.

A grave digger stepped forward to fill in the rest of the dirt. He removed his hat and performed his duty in silence. When he was done, he took off his gloves and, with his bare hands, he carefully patted and smoothed the top of the small mound. Then, dusting the grave from his knees, he donned his cap, picked up his shovel, and left as silently as he had worked.

From behind her grief, Marika had felt the beauty and witnessed the love and care that the town was expressing toward her brother. But her heart could not respond with anything other than loss.

At midnight the night before, when she had felt her brother's passing, she had run in the darkness to the barn. Hidden in the corner of a stall, she allowed herself to weep. Somewhere near the house a man was singing, and she took as much comfort from it as she was capable of at the time. A gray and white cat with two kittens had climbed into her lap; she was only vaguely aware of their soft warm attempts to share her sorrow, purring to comfort and console the best way they knew.

That morning, she had waited behind the barn until the procession was well on its way toward the cemetery. Cautioning Scout to stay behind, she had then followed the people at a distance.

From tree to tree she had crept within the cemetery walls. Shadow to shadow. No sound from under her feet. Not even her breath competed with the wind.

Crouched low behind a large headstone guarded by a glorious grieving angel of rich white marble, Marika waited until the last mourner left. Then the workman. Even then, she watched until the shadows lengthened and the stillness was everywhere. A dove called to its mate. The breeze stirred the blossoms that surrounded Danny's grave.

With an explosion of pent-up grief and guilt, Marika flew from her hiding place and cast her young body across the grave. She wept until her tears soaked the fresh earth. The rocks cut into her cheek. Dirt clung to her lips. Her knees pulled up in reflex to her body's wrenching sorrow.

When at last her tears were spent and her heart was empty, she lay without moving as near to her brother as she could be until dawn.

Then, as the sun was cresting over the edge of the field east of the cemetery, Marika felt a warmth settle down over her aching body. From a distance above her she heard the words: "Come child. It's time to go."

She looked up into the kind black face of Joseph, and felt his coat covering her. But by the time she had raised herself to her knees, he was already walking away. She steadied herself and began to walk behind him, following at least ten feet away, in silence.

He stopped in front of Maggie Nydegger's house, and waited for her to catch up to him.

"She's a good woman," he said. "You can let her see you."

Marika handed him back his coat, and they parted. She watched him walk down the lane toward town. She considered the house in front of her, and then she headed toward the barn – stealthily from tree to tree, moving in silence and shadow. Unseen.

THE FARM.

When Marika was safely enveloped within the barn's dark, cool interior, she became very aware of the hunger aching inside her belly. She tried to remember the last time she ate. Yesterday, perhaps, or the day before. The last of her cheese and bread brought from Boston. An apple. She remembered choking it down between prayers for Danny's soul, sharing bits with the cats. Could it have been just yesterday? She felt ages older than when she last clutched Danny's hand, ruffled his silk-like hair through her fingers, smelled his nearness.

Her vision swam in tears and her pale cheeks felt their warm, wet comfort again. But her stomach distracted her thoughts and competed with her broken heart for attention. She sighed brokenly, deeply, and with it caught the unmistakable smell of freshly baked yeast bread.

From the barn door, across the glistening paddock, she could see an open kitchen window, its white starched curtains fluttering. On the wide wooden window ledge, several loaves were cooling. Marika was there and back in the tick of a clock. Only slight imprints in the dew-topped paddock grass gave evidence of her passing, and they were drying quickly in the rising sun. And now there were three loaves, where once there had been four. Scout watched with contemplative interest from a field behind the barn, then returned to his morning hunt.

Marika carefully laid the golden treasure on a step of the ladder leading up to the hayloft; just above was the soft hideaway where she had finally slept the night Danny died.

With gratitude for the early hour, she saw that the cow had not yet been milked.

She lifted a wooden milk pail from a peg and pulled a sturdy three-legged stool from its perch, all the while singing softly – a Gaelic child's tune, a calming sort of lullaby.

Marika's singing was to hear the voices of blessed angels. Her music surrounded you, caressed your heart, your mind, the palms of your hands, the soles of your feet. You *felt* her song inside you. It was a gift from her father who, it was said, "could sing copper into gold, and the soul right out of a body."

Marika smiled then, the first in a long time. She thought of her "Da." She could hear his laugh, his songs, in his melodious clear tenor. As far back as she could remember, she knew his voice and his singing. She well knew the way he could captivate any audience – around a campfire under a star-filled sky, or around a pint in a smoke-filled pub for enough coins to buy her and Gran and Danny a bit of treat each.

And she knew just as well that it was her father's songs and his laughter, his charm and wit that had wooed and seduced her mother. A woman of fine family and upbringing she was. Not one of them. She was from an old, respected Boston family of wealth and privilege. A family refined out of all its character and heart, her grandmother would say and spit into the fire.

Da had told Marika how much he and her mother had loved each other. And how the two families had recoiled at their union. Marriage was never a choice or a chance. He told her when she,

Marika, was born, he had taken her to raise by himself. She was his alone. But, somewhere in the deepest mists of Marika's memory, there was a mother's warmth, a scent, perhaps a face – and then, it was gone.

He spoke of his love with her mother, and the tragedy of it, when he had been at the pubs too long, and he wept openly, and Marika felt somehow responsible. She knew nothing to say to comfort him. She was gratified for this show of love he had felt for the mother she never knew, yet, somehow, embarrassed by it as well.

Marika had inherited her father's heavy dark hair, rich with red-gold, a mass of tangled curls. Pale, almost translucent skin, smooth to the eye and touch, like cream. And eyes so dark with thick lashes and gray-blue tinge to the lids they looked like God's thumbs had smudged them with coal. But the one thing of her mother's that Marika would have forever was the hue of her eyes. While Marika's Irish blood would have provided her with deep clear blue or perhaps even green eyes, hers were so pale a blue they were almost white, yet rough-edged in black, making the blue within them even more startling. Marika learned long ago she could fix those eyes on someone and mesmerize their very soul. Her grandmother also realized their significance, and felt the "gift" in her as well. So, for thirteen years, she had nurtured and trained and coaxed Marika's gifts to her consciousness and control. Even then, Marika was still discovering her full potential.

While Gran was cultivating Marika's mystic abilities, Da taught her his songs. And Marika singing wove spells as surely as any Gran could teach her.

Marika sang for her "*thribli*" (her family or clan) often and willingly. Sometimes, Da would make her sing for the "others," when he needed street money or a distraction. But, for the most part, Marika sang only for herself – and Danny. She sang to explore her feelings and complete her thoughts. She sang to take leave of herself. She sang to disappear into the natural world that she loved too well, to become a part of the very trees and grass and wind. She sang to sit on the lap of God. And now, she sighed, she was singing like a common woman of the street for her breakfast. But its effect was real enough and needed, lulling the cow into contentment and relaxation, ready to accept a stranger's touch.

The bucket placed under the udder, herself seated on the small stool, her head leaned gently against the animal's flank, she crooned softly and began the rhythmic milking. She easily took three bucketsful of thick, creamy liquid and poured each into a waiting pottery milk jug.

She held back a few cups of the warm frothy milk and took it over to the hayloft ladder where the bread awaited. There she sat, cross-legged on the floor. She dunked the fresh bread into the milk and soon contented her stomach. Milk-soaked pieces of bread placed on the dirt floor next to her filled the cats with purrs.

When at last she felt satisfied, she remembered the strawberry plants behind the house. She studied the cottage for a long moment, then stole her way to the garden. She could see and smell wood-smoke rising from the chimney.

Behind her, a young boy approached the barn from across the field to its south. He was whistling a nonsense sort of tune. Swinging the barn door open wide, he sauntered in. Marika crawled behind a grapevine that was curling its way over a small trellis at the edge of the garden. Peering through the web of its woody stems, she watched the boy leave the barn after just a few minutes. He had pulled the large milk jug to the barn door. Then, looking toward the house, he waved his hand high over his head, turned, and retraced his steps across the field, whistling his same tuneless music.

Marika grinned at the confusion she had probably created. And then she turned her attention to the strawberry patch just in front of her. She filled her mouth with the firm, sweet fruit, and loaded her pockets and skirt front with as many more as she could pick.

A slight sound reached her. Movement within the house. She ducked and ran to the barn. She headed to the loft ladder and clutched her skirt full of berries to her chest as she climbed the steps to her hideaway. She shuffled through the hay to the pulley door and ventured a look out. From her vantage point she could see both the front and back of the cottage as well as the paddock and garden.

Marika sucked the juice from another berry, then saw Maggie come out the back door, cross the porch, and walk the paths of the garden looking closely at the strawberry plants. The old woman returned to the house, disappearing inside; she reappeared out the front door, a large woven basket over her arm that was filled with something and covered with a white cloth. She headed in the direction of town.

A nagging alarm crept across the back of Marika's neck as she remembered the two carpetbags she had thrust under the back porch and never retrieved.

She turned to descend. There, under the roofline as it met the floor of the loft, placed neatly side-by-side, were the two bags.

"Damnú air!" the Gaelic oath leapt unbidden from her tongue. She made the sign of the cross over her mouth.

Who had seen her and when? She would have to leave. But she had not yet made up her mind about where she would go. Her sense of family pushed at her, telling her she should be honor-bound to complete her original journey – to the waiting community of local Irish Travellers and gypsies. Da had made a contract. Da had made promises to one of their leaders, one considered a prince. A man not to be crossed. Her father had pledged that she would take the man for her husband. She was just reaching her age. And when her grandmother had passed, there was no one to claim that Marika was needed with them in Boston with the rest of the O'Hara *thribli* – the only family the young innocent had ever known.

Marika had pleaded with Da to let Danny be the one to accompany her. Tradition demanded she not make the trip alone; but it was she who had chosen her baby brother to come with her. She wanted to know someone was looking after him properly. And yet, it was she who had let him down in the end. She who had somehow allowed his death. Her broken heart enabled this unholy thought to float to the surface. "It's my fault!" she wailed to God. "Danny, forgive me; Father, forgive me," she chanted.

A fierceness rose up in her throat. "*I will be the one to choose now. I will not go to him.*" Fear slid ice around her heart. "But where will I go? Where will I hide? I must find a place – a place to wait, to think, to decide."

Frantically, irrationally, her eyes darted around the hay loft. She picked up her bags and set them down again. She walked in circles, one hand tangling her hair. Then, she remembered Joseph's words from that morning: "*She's a good woman. You can let her see you.*" She remembered the care and compassion Maggie had shown to Danny. But to take that chance was more fear-filled for Marika than leaving her family in Boston for the unknown in this world of Southern strangers and strangeness.

Marika gathered and clutched her strawberries in her skirt again and climbed down the ladder steps. She deposited the fruit in one of the empty milk pails. She pushed open the barn door wide enough to roll the waiting pottery milk jug through it, then continued rolling it on a zigzag journey to the foot of the back porch steps of the cottage. She repeated the trip a few minutes later with the pail of strawberries.

It was several hours before Maggie Nydegger returned home. The sun was high. Marika had been dozing in the hay loft, playing with the kittens. She had tossed a stick for Scout. She had taken the cow out to the fields, and released the horse to the paddock to graze. She had found a wire basket and gathered eggs from the hen house, placing it, too, at the back porch door. She had scattered corn around the ground to the flurry of clucking and flapping of flightless wings. And then she had walked carefully through each room of the cottage, lifting, touching, but returning articles exactly as they had lain. There were, however, two exceptions. A small silver sewing thimble had caught her eye, just at the top of a wicker basket full of mending on a table next to a short armless rocking chair. Marika slid it neatly into her pocket. In the bedroom upstairs, she found a grand, gold pocket watch in a drawer of the large mahogany dresser. She held it to her ear. No tick. But lovely and heavy and glorious to hold. She ran her fingers over its intricate carving, and thought of Da. This, too, found its way into Marika's pocket.

In her own mind, Marika had not yet made a conscious decision to stay where she was. But she had discerned no alternatives that seemed better. So she returned to the barn to simply wait, not certain of what she might be waiting for.

Maggie walked into the cottage through the front door, then came out onto the back porch. She walked slowly around the gathered goods that Marika had placed there, then quickly over to the barn and searched its interior with her eyes. She came out, shaded her gaze from the sun, and looked across the fields. She returned to the house. She never spoke a word.

By early evening, the young whistling boy had come and gone, herding the cow back to the barn and milking her. He had hurriedly, half-heartedly, mucked the stalls and brought the horse in from the paddock. He had toted the milk buckets to the house – spilling as much as he carried, Marika noted with disdain – and placed them on the back porch. He had knocked at the door and spoken briefly to Maggie, shaking his head to her obvious questions.

Long, deep shadows were reaching into night when Marika crept near the house again to see if she could find or learn anything more of use to her. At the edge of the back porch, she discovered some of her brother's clothing washed and folded neatly in a small pile resting on his thin brown shoes. Across the top lay the St. Christopher medal. She picked up the small medallion, kissed it softly, then dropped it into her pocket. She touched the jacket, fingering its small tin buttons, and remembered how Da had made them and Gran had sewn them on. The jacket itself had been found at the edge of a field. But Gran and Da had made it special for Danny with the brightly polished, hand-crafted buttons. How proud Danny had been of that coat.

Marika impulsively reached out and systematically broke the threads holding the buttons to the coat, putting them one-by-one into the same pocket that now held the St. Christopher.

Gradually, as the darkness was settling, Marika became aware of a soft glow emanating from the windows of the house. She was crouched low next to the back porch, just outside the window of the room where Danny had been taken. A voice floated out from the open kitchen window, above and to the left of her head: "If you'd like to have something hot to eat, just come in through the back door."

Without really deciding, Marika stood up and walked across the back porch, waiting silently before the door. The voice called out again: "It's not going to stay hot all night."

Marika lifted the latch and pushed the door open just wide

enough to see in with one eye. No one was there. Danny's cot had been stripped down to its rope frame and moved against the wall. It helped her to not remember.

The sound of a dish being filled with a ladle floated from the other side of the brick fireplace – along with very compelling smells. She heard the ladle being returned to the pot on the stove.

"Would you like some more milk, as well?"

Marika's head peered around the brick wall and saw Maggie just sitting down at a table in the center of the room. It was a thick, square table, made of solid oak and scrubbed almost white, but no cloth covered it. Two plates, two cups, two spoons, were aligned on opposite sides. From her seat, Maggie began slicing a large slab of bread from a loaf similar to the one Marika had taken earlier from the windowsill.

Maggie put the knife down and lifted a pottery jug from the center of the table. She poured smooth white milk into a cup waiting for Marika across the table from herself. "This milk's cold. It's been in the spring house. Do you like milk cold?" Maggie spoke to Marika as if they were equals, as if she were waiting for her to be seated at the same table, to share the same food.

Marika stepped into the room shyly, her chin feigning confidence. Although she had been in the cottage earlier, her eyes took in the entire kitchen in a single sweep again: from the glowing fire at the hearth to the top of the cook stove, where the source of a warm and tempting aroma steamed softly into the room. She had been taught from an early age to observe all things quickly and thoroughly, and she noted everything during her few measured steps from around the back of the fireplace to the side of the table.

She waited to be told what to do, still disbelieving that the woman intended for her to sit at the table. Maggie dispelled that concern promptly: "Go ahead ... sit down ... eat," she motioned to the place and plate opposite herself. Soup filled the bowl and milk brimmed the cup.

Marika slid sideways into the sturdy ladder-back chair without moving it. Her feet dangled and she hooked her legs around the chair's crossbar. She kept her hands folded tightly in her lap.

The two dinner companions indulged in a long judgmental look at one another.

At last, Maggie broke the silence and said, smiling, "Bow your head, child, so I can say the blessing."

Marika believed she anticipated what would come next – she would be asked to sing for her meal. And so she stood beside her chair, saying, "I will sing the blessing, if you'd like, Miss."

Maggie was somewhat taken aback, but nodded in agreement. She bowed her head. And Marika sang.

Amazing Grace, how sweet the sound
That saved a wretch like me.
I once was lost but now am found,
Was blind, but now I see.

'Twas Grace that taught my heart to fear,
And Grace my fears relieved.
How precious did that Grace appear
The hour I first believed.

Through many dangers, toils and snares
We have already come.
'Twas Grace that brought us safe thus far,
And Grace will lead us home.

The Lord has promised good to me,

His word my hope secures.
He will my shield and portion be,
As long as life endures.

When we've been here ten thousand years,
Bright shining as the sun.
We've no less days to sing God's praise
Than when we've first begun.

Not sure of what Maggie expected, Marika sang all the verses she knew. She then stood quietly for Maggie to respond. At the first few notes, Maggie had held her breath for the beauty and spirituality of it. There were tears in her eyes as she looked at Marika with absolute awe and appreciation for the gift this young girl had just given to her. She forgot to speak.

Marika eventually asked: "May I eat now, please, Miss?"

"Oh, my, yes!" Maggie struggled to find words. "The blessing was lovely," she said finally.

"Thank you, Miss." Marika picked up her spoon and began to taste the tantalizing soup. It was a thick, creamy, chicken stock full of vegetables Maggie had harvested and put-up the summer before. The fresh bread that Maggie had sliced and was handing over to her was spread liberally with new butter.

"Who taught you to sing like that?" Maggie asked.

"My Da taught me the song, but my singing just comes from inside me," Marika replied. "It comes from the place where God's living, Gran used to say."

"I think your Gran is right ... very right, indeed," Maggie said quietly.

They ate in silence for a bit. Then Maggie began to ask the girl questions: "Where do you come from?"

Marika thought for a moment before answering. Without a trace of disrespect or guile, she said quite simply: "Not here."

Maggie said: "Where are your Da and Gran now?"

"Gran's in Heaven. Da's not."

This was a child who had been taught to keep herself to herself, Maggie thought, but then said: "How about telling me your name?"

Marika did not answer, but just continued to eat her soup.

"Perhaps I could just keep calling you 'Child'?" Maggie prodded her.

Marika considered the possibility for a bit and then replied, "You can call me Callín, then." She pronounced it "Colleen."

Marika spoke with the lyrical yet telling lilt of the Irish that pleased Maggie's ear. And she also recognized that "Colleen" in Irish simply meant "girl."

Her tone was serious when Maggie tried one more question: "Was the sick little boy that Doc Jackson brought to me the other day traveling with you?"

The suddenness of the question startled Marika and tears came unchecked to her eyes. She tried to look down quickly, but Maggie had seen the abject grief in them. She knew immediately that she had hit upon the truth.

Marika dropped her spoon into the bowl and half darted from the chair. But something in the kindness of Maggie's face and demeanor kept her there. She took a deep breath and answered just loudly enough for Maggie to hear: "Yes. My brother."

"I'm sorry, Child," Maggie whispered back. "I'm so sorry that you lost him. Doc tried to help him – we all did. And I was holding his hand at the end. He wasn't alone."

"I know," Marika said, and then looked Maggie full in the eyes. "Thank you."

Maggie reached across the table and took Marika's hand in her own. It felt small and thin and quivered pitifully. "Would you tell me the boy's name?" she asked.

Marika shook her head in silence. "We're not supposed to ever tell 'others' our real names," she explained. "We are christened one name, you see – then we're given another name to be called out loud. It's a sort of 'nick name'. It keeps our family protected. I'm sorry. It's just our way," she ended abruptly.

Maggie could not press the matter further. "Well, then, what can I call him? What was his 'nick name'?"

"You could call him 'Mac'," Marika answered. And Maggie understood the Irish word for "son."

A frightening possibility hit Marika then, and she said, "Please, please – you must not put a stone on his grave using a name. Do you promise me?"

"Yes, of course," Maggie calmed the girl. "There is a headstone being prepared right now for him – but it only says The Little Boy, 1855. Will that be all right? It's a very small one. The town is paying for it."

Marika nodded her assent. The Travellers would not find her through that, she believed. Yes, that would keep their presence secret enough.

They finished their meal, each tucked within her own thoughts. Maggie had baked a fresh strawberry pie – from the fruit picked by Marika. They had slices covered in cream.

"Was it you who stole a loaf of my bread this morning?" Maggie asked suddenly.

"I did pay you for it," Marika defended.

"How did you pay? With what?" Maggie replied.

"I left you milk and strawberries and eggs for it," Marika reminded her.

"But they were *my* strawberries, *my* eggs – milk from *my* cow,"

Maggie half laughed at her.

"Ah, and those berries sure weren't pickin' themselves now, were they? And the cow didn't just walk over and leave her milk at your doorstep, just as you please. And no hen that I saw came up and laid her egg in the basket." Marika's logic was defensive but pure.

Maggie had to laugh. "Yes, you did do me a service in payment for the bread, I have to say." She chuckled again as she began to clear the table.

Marika carried her own dish to the washing-up tub, while Maggie lifted a large kettle that had been boiling on the stove and poured its contents over the dishes in the tub. She took a clean cloth and wiped the dishes in the hot water, then put them in the rack over the sink to drip dry.

Marika had retaken her seat at the table.

"Tell me about him," Maggie said to the girl as she put the last dish up. "Tell me about your brother. He was so fair of hair, compared to you. You didn't look much alike."

"My brother was a secret child," Marika answered simply. "Da and Gran took him to live with us."

"Your family just took a child?" Maggie asked bluntly, and rather too sharply. She had suspected that the girl was a gypsy. This confirmed it. And the rumors and fears. Children were hidden at the very sight of a gypsy wagon or caravan. Kidnappings – sons and daughters secreted away from in front of their own homes or walking to school, and never seen again.

Marika understood exactly what Maggie was thinking and responded explosively: "No, no. We don't take children – not like that. No, Miss. We love children. We take only the ones who are *given* to us."

"Who on earth would give their child away?" Maggie was incredulous.

"Now, Miss," Marika started to explain in a voice suited for speaking to someone of little intelligence. "Haven't you known of some nice rich girl – someone of good family, but who thinks too much of herself by half? And haven't you known her to like the lads just a bit too much? And hasn't she then gone off to visit her Aunt in the next town over, or some faraway village, or even abroad if they've enough money for it? And who do you think takes the child, then? Who raises it like their own and loves it and teaches it to pray and the like? Those are the 'secret' children. That was my brother. And I loved him ever so much."

"I'm sorry," Maggie said with humility. "I didn't know ... didn't think. And I'm sure you did love your brother very much. I am sorry."

"That's all right, Miss. You weren't to know. Most don't."

Once she had started talking about Danny, Marika seemed to want to go on. "My brother was always a wee one," she started, "and I helped Gran take care of him all his life. Did you feel his hair? Just like a kitten it was – so soft and light, and bright as the moon. He was a good boy. Never a bit of trouble. But when Gran passed, I knew I had to keep him with me to watch out for him." Marika took a ragged breath, "But I didn't take good care of him, did I?" She looked at Maggie with longing for comfort.

Maggie was overwhelmed with sympathy. The girl in front of her was just a child. How could she be expected to take care of herself as well as her brother?

Maggie reached toward Marika tentatively, saying consolingly, "You did just fine, Child. You can't go blaming yourself. Even Doc Jackson couldn't make him well – and he can fix just about anybody with just about any ailment."

Marika moved hesitantly into Maggie's outstretched arms, and heard her whisper the words she most needed to hear: "It wasn't your fault ... it wasn't your fault at all."

They sat quietly together. The darkness settled around the little cottage. Maggie lighted candles and two small whale oil lamps. The fireplace itself provided the primary illumination.

Marika curled on the floor at Maggie's feet with her head in the older woman's lap. Maggie caressed her hair and they spoke little.

Scout had crept in at some point and lay near the fire, ready to protect his two humans. His ears cocked, he listened to their talk, dozing in their comfort and company.

With a sudden thought, Marika raised her head and said, "Thank you for washing my brother's clothes."

"You're welcome," Maggie said simply. "Would you like to wash your clothes, too?" she then asked. Was the girl leading up to that very request?

"No, Miss, I don't believe I would. But I wouldn't mind a wash of my own, if that wouldn't be too much trouble. I've been thinking I've been smelling a bit of the barn."

"Now that you mention it ..." Maggie confessed.

"Well, Miss, it's your barn, now, isn't it?" Marika responded.

"Why don't you just call me Maggie – or Magdalena?" Maggie invited.

"It wouldn't seem right now, would it? Me calling you by your Christian name, and you not knowing mine," Marika said with a slow smile.

Marika went to the well and drew the water. Maggie heated it on the stove and poured it into a large tin tub she had brought out of the corner. She thought about how old women need to be needed.

The young girl hesitated slightly before undressing. Maggie discretely left the room. She came back in to assist with pouring fresh water over the thin body in the tub, and realized what a child she really still was. Not a hint of a woman about her yet.

Another bit of the gypsy culture was clawing at Maggie's heart. Was this poor thing to be married off? Is that where she and her brother were headed when he became so ill?

She posed the question to Marika, just as she wrapped her in a large warm towel and sat her down in front of the fire to dry her hair.

"Yes, Miss," was all Marika would say at first. But slowly, she unfolded her story a bit at a time.

"I've been promised to a man – a great man of an important *thribli.*"

"What does that mean?" Maggie asked.

"A family – a clan," Marika explained. "I think I shouldn't be telling you this," she expressed with regret and hesitation.

"I promise, child – *Colleen* – I won't say anything to anyone," Maggie pledged.

"He's a prince, a leader. It's a great honor for my Da. And he paid Da a lot of money. It's because of my singing that he asked for me. Lots of men asked. But Da chose this man right out from the rest. He said he would be good to me. He'd wait until I was ready to give me children. He'd buy me lots of jewelry and all the things I wanted. And he'd only make me sing when I wanted to, as well. I didn't actually believe all of it, though, Miss. You know what men are like." She sighed in childish sophistication. And too much understanding. And Maggie was alarmed.

"Surely, you're much, much too young to be married – or even promised to anyone," Maggie replied.

"We are promised when we reach our age," Marika tried to explain. "You know, just before we become a woman," Marika finished in a whisper. "It's to protect us from other men who might want us just for their pleasure. If we're married, then we're safe."

Grown men marrying little girls, Maggie thought in silent sickness. Marika answered as if the words had been spoken aloud, "It's our way, Miss. It's always been our way."

Marika had said all of this with absolute innocence, but a wistfulness as well. Maggie wondered if the girl would confide in her about what she had yet to reveal.

"Why haven't you gone on to be with your intended husband, Child?" Maggie asked with unexpected insight. She walked over to the fireplace and stirred the wood to new life.

Marika gazed into the fire for a long time, then. "I'm deciding."

"Well, you can stay here as long as you want while you're doing your deciding," Maggie offered.

"Thank you, Miss," Marika said; and then she stood and began to dress again.

"Don't you want a nightshirt?" Maggie asked. "I could make a bed up for you in the little room behind the fireplace."

"Oh, no, Miss," Marika responded with dismissal. "I'm right at home in the barn loft. The kittens will be wondering where I've been off to all this time. And the cow and the horse as well. We get along just fine, we do."

"Well, please take a blanket," Maggie offered.

"Thank you, Miss, I will at that."

Marika left as she had entered through the back door. Over her shoulder, she called back to Maggie, who was watching her from the porch: "It's Marika, Miss ... my name is Marika. It seems to me if you've been seeing me as bare as the day I was born, you ought to be knowing my name."

The majority of the next day passed in quiet routine. Marika kept herself hidden from all but Maggie, and helped around the farm. Maggie sold her baked goods in town for extra income; but her husband, a carpenter of superior talent and reputation, had provided well for her before his death. They had no children that lived.

Late that afternoon, Marika heard a buggy approaching. She slipped out the back door and crouched near the corner of the porch.

"Marika ...? What's wrong?" Maggie called after her.

"What's wrong with who?" Doc Jackson's voice boomed through the living room. His long strides soon brought him into view.

"Oh! I never heard you coming. I was just talking to Scout, who apparently didn't hear you either," she frowned. The dog sat enigmatically sweeping the floor with his tail, alternating his gaze between them.

"Can you help with this?" Doc Jackson then asked without any preliminary, as he handed Maggie a piece of paper with his handwriting scrawled across it.

"It's something I want to try with young Angus Knox. That bad foot of his isn't healing. And those store-bought concoctions aren't worth the tins they put 'em in," he said with disgust. "He'll be losing that foot to gangrene soon – I'll have to take it if I can't get the infection cleared up. I want to try something I've been thinking about for awhile, and I'd like your opinion." He moved around behind her so he could look over her shoulder at the paper she was now studying.

For the next several minutes, they conversed in words and phrases that Marika, listening at the window, could not understand. But she recognized the respect with which Doc Jackson was speaking to Maggie, seeking her thoughts, probing her knowledge. Marika had flashes of the way folks used to come to her Gran for her special skills, the deference they used; but also the way they pandered to her and covered her with false compliments when they wanted something from her. This was different, Marika knew. This was an expression of equality between two human beings who deeply respected each other.

"I'd give it a try," Maggie said then to the doctor. "It's good science, Walt – good thinking on your part. Need any help preparing it?"

"Thanks, Maggie," Doc Jackson replied. "I just feel better having you look it over. I think I've got all I need to compound it. Thanks."

"Keep me advised, yes?"

"Absolutely."

"Cup of tea before you leave?" Maggie offered.

"Ah ... yes, sure. That sounds fine," the doctor said.

Marika could hear the scrape of one of the chairs being pulled from the table as the doctor was seating himself.

"No more news about the little boy," Doc spoke with a sadness in his voice.

"No."

"I wish we could at least find a family to notify – either where he came from or where he was going," he said as he cooled his tea in his saucer. He poured it back into the cup, then drank almost all of it in one long swallow.

"Yes," Maggie said simply. "But I do have the feeling that he must have been loved."

"Mmmm," Doc grunted. "They put him on a train alone and sick."

"Still. He was treasured by someone, I'm sure."

"Whatever you say, Miss Maggie. Whatever you say." Doc rose to his feet and folded the paper with the medicinal notes, putting it back into his vest pocket.

"Thanks again, Maggie – for the tea and the professional consultation. The scientific community doesn't know what it's missing without you being a part of it. It's not right, you know."

"No. It's not right," Maggie agreed. "But there it is. And here you are – my good friend who helps me keep my wits sharp." (*And who makes an old woman feel needed,* she thought for the second time in as many days.)

"I'll let you know how it goes," he promised.

Doc leaned down and scratched Scout on the top of his head. Smiling broadly, he said, "Good watch dog, Scout ... good job!"

Both humans and dog walked to the front door. Marika heard one set of footsteps returning. She raised herself up to peer into the window. Maggie called out: "It's safe. Come on back in. Have some tea."

Marika sat at the kitchen table watching out of the window as the late-day shadows lengthen. "What did you help Doc with?" she asked finally.

"Something to do with medicine," Maggie answered.

"Why did he ask *you?*" the girl pursued.

"Because I happen to be a rather good scientist," Maggie replied. "In fact, I wanted to be a doctor myself."

"Why aren't you, then?"

"Because I'm a woman. And a Quaker," she tried to explain as succinctly as she could.

Marika shook her head and looked quizzically at the older woman.

With a deep sigh, Maggie leaned back in her chair, stirred the tea in her cup and watched the ripples, remembering. Without rancor, but with the inherent sadness of regret, Maggie talked of her upbringing as a young lady in the South. She had been taught just enough about a myriad of topics to allow her to converse intelligently in polite society, and no more. Her brother had been encouraged in math and sciences, while she had been expected to excel in – and content herself with – the arts. At night, she secretly read his textbooks with a hunger he never possessed. She even began tutoring him on the subjects she found so fascinating, and he could barely grasp. All the wonders of the human body and health and disease and healing were her particular passion.

Marika waited silently while Maggie relived her youthful dreams aloud.

"My brother went to University, of course. I was sent to Europe to become a proper lady," she smiled then. "And there, I fell in love ... *twice!*" she teased as her eyes twinkled.

Marika smiled back encouraging her to continue.

"My first love was with an idea," she began. "Well, more than just one idea, it was with an entire belief, a whole doctrine. One that was full of equality and dignity for all people – men and women, all races and nationalities. And it held the idea that women could become what they wanted, could study as they wished ... that they could become doctors and scientists and ministers and more. But beyond that – beyond and beneath and over all of that – it was an idea that God lives within each one of us. Like when your Gran told you your singing comes from the place where God lives in you, Marika. I truly believe that. And I learned that from the Society of Friends – the Quakers. This was the church I had to belong to! I became fascinated and convinced that this was the truth for me. But Quakers were often discriminated against back then – especially when it came to higher education. And then ... well, then, I fell in love again," Maggie's smile deepened and her face glowed with forgotten youth. "His name was John. John Nydegger. He was already a member of the Friends church. And he became my beloved husband," she finished as she looked down, her eyes veiled behind her lashes. "Suddenly, my life was filled with building a home and business together, and starting a family. And Father ... Father never forgave either of us. I had made my choices, he said.

And I was to live with them without his support or understanding or love. It broke my heart, of course. Decisions often do. And so, my dreams of becoming a doctor were gone forever."

Maggie sighed deeply again, and she absently began lighting candles to dispel the shadows streaking across her heart as well as the kitchen floor.

Marika thought through it all. Her unspoiled naivety recognized the absurdity of how Maggie had been discounted simply because she had been born a woman, and how she had been forced to make choices between family and learning and God. And yet, her personal understanding of the harsh realities of the world allowed her to believe the truth of it.

"But Doc comes to you to help him, anyway," she said eventually. "*He* can see all of you."

"Yes," Maggie said with understanding. *"He can see all of me."*

Just after they finished clearing the supper dishes, Maggie invited: "Would you like to come to our church meeting tomorrow?" She had been thinking long and hard about it. "We'll be meeting here at my house at about ten o'clock in the morning. You'd be safe. These are good people. We all trust each other with our lives."

Marika's eyes told Maggie she would refuse.

"You know Joseph, don't you? He'll be here. He's one of us," Maggie disclosed.

Marika's head came up with that. "Perhaps I'll be passing by about that time," she said. "Perhaps I'll just be looking in to see what I think."

"Good," Maggie said with obvious pleasure. "We practice a programmed worship service, and we start with the singing of hymns. I do hope you can join us for that."

Marika understood that she would be asked to perform. But her growing fondness for the older woman overcame any sense of imposition.

"Oh, look what I've found. You must have dropped this, Miss," Marika said as she reached beneath her chair to the kitchen floor. She opened her hand and revealed within it a small, silver thimble.

Marika awoke early the next morning and began to dress for church.

For all her desire to please Maggie, to impress Maggie's friends, to present herself in her best appearance, the young girl was woefully unaware of the vast differences between their two cultures, especially with regard to attire.

Marika dug through her carpetbags and found her brightest colored ribbons. She let her hair loose from its braid and, in a mass of curls, tossed it down her back and spread it across her shoulders, winding the ribbons throughout it. She pulled on a vivid blue skirt and deep red blouse. She slid on all the bracelets and necklaces that Da had painstakingly made for her of tin and his finest craftsmanship. In her ultimate, innocent expression of humility and respect, she covered her head with the precious lace her Gran had given her for her wedding day. And then, she bared her feet and ankles.

At the bottom of her bag, she found one more treasure that Gran had bestowed upon her just before she died, and she rouged her cheeks and mouth bright crimson. Without a reflection to guide her, or more experienced hands, this final effect was rather startling against her pale childish skin.

Her heart was dancing with anticipation while she silently waited until the buggies and people on foot seemed to have all arrived at the cottage. Then she ran, her heart beating, to the back door. The singing had begun. Someone was playing the piano. Marika slid with ease into the small back room, crept on her toes through the kitchen, and presented herself with joy beside the group gathered in the living room. There she waited, against the traditional Quaker blacks and grays and understated garments of all the rest of those present.

Joseph saw her first. "Lord, almighty," he said just under his breath. His immediate impulse was to grab her and race with her out of the room. But his second inclination, which hit almost as immediately, was his appreciation for her innocence and unpretentiousness. He knew in his heart, however, not all in the room that morning would see her soul as clearly as he did. Not right away, at least. Kind as these people were – accepting and all-inclusive – this vulnerable young girl was bound to be hurt.

He caught Maggie's eye and looked in the direction of the girl. Maggie's eyes widened. She stopped singing. The others followed the gaze of both Maggie and Joseph and there were terrible gasps, then humiliating silence.

Marika froze. Her hands turned to ice. Her face burned. She held Maggie's stare the longest. Then looked at Joseph. She turned and ran, with Joseph close behind.

"Wait, Colleen," she heard Maggie's voice. But it was too late. The betrayal was unforgiven.

Marika slammed through the front door and began circling the house, shouting a mixture of Irish and Shelta oaths and curses.

Then she stopped, circled more slowly, pressed her hands against the house walls themselves, chanting and commanding – words her grandmother taught her, to make the inhabitants forget, to make herself unseen once again.

Joseph was trying to intercept her as she ran, but her anger was like a fire around her, raging, unquenchable, unapproachable.

Marika suddenly broke away from her spell-casting and ran to the barn, throwing the door open wide, disappearing into its darkness. Moments later, she came riding out at full gallop on the back of Maggie's horse, her carpetbags slung on either side. She rode without a saddle or bridle, but the horse responded to her every direction. She clutched his mane in tight, angry fists, dug her knees into his sides with fierce determination, spat commands into his flattened ears.

She was disappearing over the crest of the field when Joseph returned to the house. Most of the inhabitants were dazed and wondering what had happened. Only vague memories were left. Marika's chants had hit their mark. All but one.

Maggie sat on one of the chairs, her hands beating against the sides of her head in agony. "God, forgive me," she wailed. "What have I done?"

Marika rode without slowing her pace or intensity. Her tears made halos around the trees and fences and cattle she passed. The sun hurt her head. Her spirit was teetering, on the brink of shattering. Maggie had betrayed her.

The horse pulled up hard as Marika threw herself to the ground at the edge of Danny's grave. She fell on her knees and bent double with her arms pressed against her body. And she wept with him once again, this time for a different kind of tortured loss.

Joseph found her instinctively and not long after she arrived. He walked to her side and sat beside her without speaking. Her tears had ceased, but the artificial rouge on her cheeks and lips was streaked with a grotesque reflection of the pain she was experiencing inside. He handed her a handkerchief in silence and waited until she wiped her face and blew her nose.

"Oh Joseph," she began, then stopped.

"I know, Child," was all he needed to say. "Where will you go now?"

"I don't know."

"There is a woods. Some says it's a magical one, filled with spirits," he offered.

She peered up through tear-clogged lashes. "Where?"

"Not far."

"Will you show me?"

"Yes, Child."

Marika stood and pulled her carpetbags down to the ground from the back of the horse. She sorted through them until she found what she was looking for. She carefully placed on Danny's grave the five tin buttons from his coat, then his silver St. Christopher. Reaching back into the lesser of the two bags, she pulled out a handful of tiny tin soldiers and lined them up in a row across the crested dirt mound. The earth was still so fresh it held the small gifts like a soft blanket.

Then she rocked back on her heels and sang in her clear angel voice for Danny. An old, old Irish lullaby. A hauntingly meaningful song:

> Sweet babe! a golden cradle holds thee,
> Shuheen sho, lulo lo!
> And soft the snow-white fleece enfolds thee,
> Shuheen sho, lulo lo!
> In airy bower I'll watch thy sleeping,
> Shuheen sho, lulo lo!
> Where branchy trees to the breeze are sweeping,
> Shuheen sho, lulo lo!

Joseph remained silent throughout the tribute. There were no words he could have said, after all.

As the final notes drifted heavenward and faded in the winds caught by the tops of the trees, Marika stood and looked at the only man she now trusted in the world: "Will you be showing me to the forest now, please?"

He stood, too, and reattached her carpetbags across the back of the horse, then he slipped a halter he had brought with him over the animal's nose and took the rope in his hand. He turned west and began leading the way. The sun warmed their backs, and Joseph spoke quietly to his small friend. "First, there's the main woods. And then there's somthin' they call the Carolina Bay."

Discoveries.

J oseph **was gone.**

He had walked with Marika a mile into the main woods, and shown her how to follow the creek past the pottery fields and into the edge of the Carolina Bay. They had said goodbye to each other with no second thoughts. The horse must be returned, they agreed. And then Joseph had watched as the young girl walked quickly, much too bravely, out of his sight. She had turned once, but he was no longer there.

Within a short time, Marika knew with instinct and certainty that she had come near the place she was seeking. She closed her eyes slowly and breathed in the succulent, scented air that surrounded her. So sweet, it was. So fragrant and foreign and filled with waiting discoveries. She could detect at least a half a dozen scents she didn't recognize. This was her first encounter with jasmine and magnolia and wisteria and so many others she would soon learn to know and cherish.

Keeping her eyes shut tightly, Marika listened to the woods. Pines whispered and sang. Oaks creaked with wisdom. Leaves rustled in restlessness and dropped seeds in their haste. A woodpecker rapped greedily for its dinner. Creatures crept along the pinestraw-covered floor and rested on branches overhead. A twig snapped in surprise.

Ever so gently, she raised her lashes and watched the constantly moving, ever-changing portrait of the forest. Above her, treetops waltzed with the sky. Bird wings stirred and glided on crests of air. The sunlight held specks of dust on its back and eddied and swirled its way between heaven and earth. Shadows kept secrets on tiptoe behind moss-ruffled trees.

Marika stretched out her arms, her hands open wide, palms up; she tilted her head back, her feet apart. She absorbed and experienced her surroundings with every surface and corner of her body and soul.

Slowly, silently, she turned toward a freshly fallen tree, its roots a tangle of hedge across the ground where it once stood. She grasped one of the exposed root-vines between the palms of her hands and rolled it firmly back and forth several times. Then, she held her hands cup-like to her face and inhaled the lingering scent. She smiled and nodded to herself with recognition.

The sound of woodpeckers tapped again overhead. She listened intently and discerned the difference. Hollow wood notes rapped and called from tree to tree, tree to tree. A bird signaled to its mate; again, and again, and again. And Marika smiled and nodded once more.

Her eyes then rested on pine cones placed at intervals around her in designs she had not seen for a very long time, but were immediately remembered. "Well done," she whispered.

To most eyes, there would have been no path to follow. But Marika saw it clearly. Soon, she was in the very heart of the forest where, just within view, just behind the next tree, the water glistened and winked. She was at the very center of the Carolina Bay.

The surface of the water was as slick and reflective as quicksilver. Dragonflies skipped across it, teasing and tempting the fish just below. The trees edging its banks preened in their reflections. A great blue heron held court in the middle of a marsh. Exotic, colored flowers thrust their blossoms up to the light and air while anchored in the water below, bridging the two worlds like sunbathing mermaids. Reeds beckoned for Marika to come nearer, nearer. She obliged without hesitation.

She began to walk the edges of the small, mystical lake until she found what she had suspected would be there. A narrow peninsula just a few yards wide jutted out into the water. She trod it inch-by-inch, confirming its integrity. Then she placed her carpetbags at its tip, and dragged fallen logs across it to enclose the end that attached the peninsula to the shore. She cleared the rest of the area of pinecones and debris, and drew intricate patterns in the earth with a stick all along the perimeter of the space she was claiming.

Then, she built a small fire within a circle of stones, and she caught fish and gathered berries and ate her fresh dinner in silence.

Finally, as the breezes settled down into evening stillness, Marika began to sing. Gaelic, magical songs that would sweeten even the bitterest of souls, and turn all but the stoniest of hearts. Her precious voice rose into the twilight – and the moon came out, the better to hear. The stars listened in silence as all the other life-forms of the forest were awash in Marika's music. None were afraid anymore. Half were quite in love with her. And Marika sensed their presence and trust in return. When at last she lay down to sleep, covered in a blanket of soft, brown leaves, with Danny's small coat cushioning her head, she knew she was safe and protected and very much where she was supposed to be.

"Good night to all the Fairies," she breathed out into the night air as she drifted into sleep. "We shall be meeting soon. Of that I am more than certain."

And, on the far side of the water, something sighed in assent.

The dawn breeze ruffled Marika's curls against her brow and the nape of her neck, waking her with a mother's tender touch. She breathed in all the forest's scents and listened to its morning song. Birds whistled and chirped and coaxed the rising sun through thickets of grasses and leaves and branches.

The girl yawned and stretched with all the vigor of youth and rolled over three times just for the joy of it. It brought her to the very edge of the Bay's pool of water. With playful fingers, she tickled the water's surface, watching the ripples laugh and jostle each other farther and farther out into the Bay.

Then she pulled herself to her knees and bent low over the water, cupping and dipping her hands deeply into the cool, clear liquid. She began to bathe her face and the sleep from her eyes. She watched the water reflect the trees above her, as they leaned in the breeze to glimpse her reflection as well.

Still gazing into the pool, she saw the clear, bright image of a face appear among the branches overhead, just above her right shoulder. A delicate face, with sparkling eyes and a cautious smile. She wiped the water from her eyes. It was still there. *A Fairy come to judge her merit!*

She rested the palms of her hands against the water's banks and continued to watch. She resisted the immediate urge to twist quickly to the right and look up into the tree limbs for the spirit itself. Marika knew her Fairy lore. She had heard more than her share of stories on early morning walks with Gran back home. And so, she counted carefully to ten. Then, quick as a darting fish, she plunged her right hand into the water and closed her fingers around the arm of the watching Fairy. A water Fairy, just as she had suspected. One skilled in the art of reflection and misdirection – something else

Marika knew a bit about from her own heritage and lifestyle.

Gripping tightly to his arm, Marika pulled the water Fairy to the surface and sat him down on a rock beside her. He sputtered, but stayed put. A Fairy, once caught, after all, is obliged to sit and visit for a bit.

"Good morning," she smiled at him, as she wiped her hands dry on her skirt.

"Morning," he answered back, noncommittally, but he pulled his forelock of hair in a nod of respect.

"And who do I have the pleasure of meeting and talking with this lovely morning?" Marika asked with the most proper manners she knew.

"Mmm. Irish, are you?" he grinned at her. "You can always tell the Irish. Takes you three times as many words to say something than most folks."

"And here I was using my best wit and words just to be polite. And you still haven't spoken your name to me," she threw back.

"Well, Irish, in your native tongue my name would be *Cian*. It means..."

"Oh, I know what it means," Marika interrupted without thought. "It means 'ancient.' So you're the ancient one, then ... the oldest in this place?" she asked, quite amazed to have made contact with someone of such importance so soon. "I'm very pleased to meet you, Cian. My name is Marika," she spoke her real name without hesitation.

"Marika? What kind of Gaelic name is that?" he responded with a snort.

"It's not. It's the name my mother gave me. She was Flemish," Marika answered.

"She gave you a name and then gave you away ... eh, Irish?" he said not cruelly. But Marika wondered how he knew.

She nodded.

"An Irish with no words. Now there's a first," he said.

It made Marika laugh. And her laughter seemed to break apart and echo all about them in the woods. Or were there separate sources for the laughter? Her eyes gleaned the trees and bushes, the brambles and vines and pinecones.

"Are there others?" she asked Cian.

"Of course, there are others," he answered.

"Others I can see, I mean?"

"Others you can see, you mean? Perhaps." He raised his voice ever so slightly, "Are there others she can see, she means?" he said with a gleeful grin.

"I suppose," a voice answered from behind a tree behind them both.

Then, from the backs of tree trunks and rocks, from under lily pads and magnolia leaves, and scrambling down from the limbs overhead, there appeared nearly a dozen more Fairies from Cian's gathering.

Marika had never imagined so many at one time, and she delighted in their individual charm and character. Not all of them came forward to meet her personally. But a few did. And, one by one, Cian introduced them to her.

The first to step out – from over the edge of a huge magnolia blossom, was Wee Ann. She was thin and willowy and she was quite discernibly the smallest of them all. She spoke in a tiny, timid voice. And then, only a few words at a time. She moved in fits and starts. Small gestures. Shy glances. But she was sweet and kind and Marika liked her immensely right from the start.

Marika was surprised, however, at how variable all the Fairies could appear in size and even solidity. Each seemed to grow larger or smaller, and intensify in clarity and opacity or fade into the merest ghost of an image – all seemly dependent on the brightness of the sunlight or the deepness of the shade or the strength of the wind at the moment. At times she thought it might be connected to how intently one was watching or listening to them. Perhaps it was just a trick of will on their own parts, she considered.

This characteristic was particularly noticeable with the one Cian introduced as Aisling. Aisling came riding into view from the very tops of the trees on a slender bit of sunbeam. Her name meant "dream" or "vision" in Irish, Marika knew. And dreams are often illusive things, she reasoned. And then she noticed how frightening this Fairy could look at one moment, yet quite benign, almost hopeful, the next. She sat in the shadows, not speaking. Watching. Waiting.

Marika discovered it was best to act slightly disinterested in the Fairies creeping about her. They looked into both her carpetbags and took turns trying on her shoes. She let them brush her long hair and wind their fingers through her curls.

While she was waiting for them to feel comfortable with her, she asked them questions about their origins. How they had come to create and inhabit this Carolina Bay in particular.

Like her own people, Marika discovered the Fairies were an ancient race. In the time before time, some had been taken from their native countries and made to work for others for little pay and even less appreciation. They were chosen from around the world for their particular skills and talents. They were visionaries and architects, poets and storytellers, musicians and artists, healers and tillers of the earth. They were well versed in magic and the mysteries of nature and could talk to animals in their own unique languages. They were not all of the same background originally. But intermarriage and social bonds brought new depths to their culture as it did even greater discrimination from outsiders.

Soon, the oppression became unbearable. The persecution went beyond unjust. They were driven into hiding. The lush forests of Europe provided for all their needs; and they became passionate defenders of personal freedom. Eventually, they refused to communicate with the others entirely. It was as if they lived *in* the same world with the others, but not *of* it. They were completely independent one from the other. Only occasionally, did the two cultures come into contact, and then, the Fairies employed their magic to the utmost. They were, for the most part, simply the "unseen." And thus they had lived for generation after generation after generation.

"But how did you come to live in the Carolina Bays and the forests of America?" Marika continued to prod.

"Curiosity," Cian said in a word. His lips shut tightly. The other Fairies all suddenly looked the other way. And, Marika believed, that was going to be a story perhaps told another day.

Even before Marika could form her next question, a sudden, startling, loud "crack" echoed all about them. Cian rolled his eyes. A long whooshing sound, followed by another ear-splitting "crack" struck even closer. Marika sat silent, quite alarmed, but the Fairies seemed to be rather unimpressed.

"Come forward, Whip," Cian commanded. Then, turning to Marika, he said, "He can sting like the Devil, as well, and never leaves a mark or so much as a shadow."

With yet a third crack – this one not nearly so threatening, yet right in front of Marika's nose – another Fairy appeared. He was laughing. A silent laugh – all teeth and shoulders and belly, but no actual sound. Marika laughed, too, and that seemed to please him. He took her hand in his, bowed over it like a true gentleman, and then bit her soundly on the knuckle. She pulled her hand away quickly, and laughed once again – loudly, looking him straight in the eye.

"Pleased to meet you, Mr. Whip," she said in a clear strong voice.

He nodded, grinned, and went to sit on a nearby log and poke at bugs.

Marika was quite enjoying herself when a gentle sound of a breaking twig and stirred leaves drew her attention from across a curve in the pond several yards away. There, standing alone, his hand against a tall pine, his face alight with joy, was her brother Danny. The sun caught the shine of his pale, almost white hair. He waved his childish hand at Marika and then held it out to her. Even the silver buttons on his tiny coat gleamed and glinted in the morning light.

Marika's heart folded in on itself. She couldn't breathe. There was a sudden ringing in her ears. And then she saw the coat – the buttons – the truth.

She closed her eyes tightly and hissed: "No, no, please ... not Danny ... anyone but Danny."

With her words, the Fairy's shape faded from Danny's image and became one of a young country girl, with braids and button shoes, a dark skirt and sweater. "I'm sorry," she called to Marika with real concern as she ran toward her. "I didn't mean to upset you. He's so strong in your mind and heart – I just shifted into his appearance quite naturally. I am sorry," she said again with sincere regret now reflected across her face.

Marika slowly opened her eyes. "A Shifter," she said quietly. "You're a Shapeshifter, aren't you?"

"Yes," the girl answered quickly. "I usually just assume the strongest image around me. I didn't mean to hurt you. Is this all right?" she motioned to herself.

"It's just too soon – I loved Danny so. He died so suddenly. And it was my fault. And now he is *only* a memory to me," Marika explained. She stopped to wipe her eyes. "But now – now, you're a good memory. A friend from my *thribli* in Boston," she reassured the Shifter.

Cian then asked, "Is that why you're here in our forest? Because of your brother's death?"

"It's a bit of the reason," she answered. She sat herself on the bank of the water then, and slid her bare feet across its cool surface, and she told the Fairies of her need to have a place to wait, to hide, to decide what she was going to do. She told them, too, about the man to whom she had been promised. And, for the first time, she said the name by which he was known: Jacko.

All the Fairies listened in silence.

Marika described her experience in town – Danny's death and Doc and Maggie and Joseph, and the Quaker meeting that Sunday. And the Fairies waited until she had quite finished.

"We know him," Cian said with great solemnity. "Jacko. He comes here to hunt."

"Cruel," Wee Ann said. "Scary to me."

Then, one by one, the Fairies began to disappear from Marika's view. Finally, she was alone. Alone to think and remember and try to decide.

Several days had passed since Marika had first met Cian and some of the other Fairies. Since then, Cian had come to see her at least once each day. And Wee Ann was there every morning to greet her with a soft Fairy kiss on her cheek, then shyly skip away. But, for the most part, the other Fairies stayed hidden or simply went about their business, not paying too much attention to the presence of this stranger.

One morning, as Marika lay with her eyes still shut, drifting gently in and out of dreams and wakefulness, she caught an unusual scent. Sweet. Almost overwhelmingly sweet. Like jasmine and honeysuckle and wisteria all gathered together in a large tight bundle warmed in the sun. She opened first one eye, then the other. Sitting much too close to her was a new Fairy – one whom Marika was sure she had never met before, yet who still looked vaguely familiar, like someone out of her past. The young Fairy had honey-colored hair and skin, and her breath wafted waves of spun sugar. She sucked on her fingers and smiled constantly. "My name is 'Yum'," she managed to say around the thumb she had planted firmly in her mouth.

"You may recognize her already," Cian broke in as he came out of the water to sit by her side. "She has a habit of lingering around babies and children ... leaves them treats in their cradles and bunting and no one can discover who brought them. She's already been caught a few times, as well," he finished with a frown and a note of displeasure in his voice.

"Of course she's been caught," spoke another Fairy unknown to Marika who suddenly appeared in their midst. "But it's all right. Children forget soon enough. And no one believes them when they do remember." Marika sat up then, not accustomed to so many strangers crowding around her as she slept.

The second newcomer turned to Marika, offering her his hand. A firm, warm handshake. "They call me 'Fixer.' I'd tell you my real name, but nobody can pronounce it. So 'Fixer' is fine. I fix things. Oh ... I suppose you could deduce that, couldn't you? I find things, too. Maybe you wouldn't know that. Fix and find. Fix and find. Nice to meet you."

"How do you do? It's very nice to make your acquaintance," Marika said, when she could.

"Fix and find," he said again and again as he nodded and backed farther and farther away until he had disappeared into the foliage.

She noticed that Yum was gone as well – although her strong, sweet scent still lingered.

The very next day, Wee Ann had already come and gone, but Cian was still having his morning visit with Marika. As was their budding custom, they chatted comfortably together while she washed her face and hands and brushed her hair. She looked around for one of her ribbons to tie at the end of her braid and soon discovered that every ribbon she owned was missing. She hated to suspect one of her new acquaintances of the theft, but they were, after all, the only ones around. She wasn't quite sure what to do or even how to address the issue with Cian.

"Here," a strange voice said abruptly and rather sullenly at her side. Yet another heretofore un-introduced Fairy had appeared so suddenly that Marika completely let loose of the end of her hair. His hand was full of her entire collection of ribbons and shook slightly. His face looked as though it had never worn a smile. And his eyes were dark and veiled.

Marika took the ribbons he held out to her and reflexively said, "Thank you."

Instantly, the new visitor fairly screamed in fury and tore the ribbons away from her. He ripped them with his teeth and fingers, flung the bits to the ground and stomped them into the dirt.

Cian quickly intervened between the furious Fairy and an astounded Marika. "Calm down, Thackeray," he said. "She wasn't to know now, was she? Just calm yourself."

As Thackeray's tantrum subsided, Cian turned to Marika, explaining, "Have you ever heard about those Fairies to whom you must never, ever, say 'thank you'?"

Marika nodded, yes.

"Well ..." Cian waved his arms at Thackeray. "There you go!" And he resumed his seat on a nearby rock, while Thackeray went stumbling and sputtering and cursing behind a tree.

"Oh, dear," Marika said looking at the remnants of her once beautiful ribbons.

But then she began collecting the clover blossoms that grew along the bank of the water, thinking she could tie them together in a chain that she could then wrap around the ends of her hair.

As she sat cross-legged on the ground and began the assembly process, she felt the unmistakable ripple across her back that meant a new presence was watching her. She looked questioningly at Cian.

"Aye," he answered. "They'll come forward soon enough. I'm surprised it's taken them this long, to be honest. Or not to be honest," he finished cryptically.

Slowly, stealthily, from behind a single, extremely gnarled and ancient cypress tree, two more Fairies eventually made their presence visible. One appeared from either side of the twisted and lump-knotted trunk.

"Nan and Bob," Cian announced them with a mere wave of his hand in their direction.

Marika hesitated to acknowledge them individually. They looked identical to one another – absolute mirror images. Which was which? Both looked male and female. Even their voices, their gestures, were without differentiation. Then, the one on the left spoke up: "I'm Nan, he's Bob."

But before Marika could respond to the clarification, the other one replied: "No...*he's* Bob, *I'm* Nan."

Cian explained, "Both are liars by birth, talent, and profession. You'll never get the truth out of either one. Or perhaps you will occasionally. But, who's to know?" he shrugged. "Even their names are the same backwards and forwards," he pointed out.

"It began eons ago, they say," Cian continued. "When one of their ancestors decided ...."

Here, Nan (or Bob) broke in, saying, "The truth is so limiting, you see. With lies there are *infinite* possibilities! How boring if we all only told the truth all the time."

"Don't you agree?" the other one asked Marika as he (or she) peered at the young girl, leaning toward her across a large rock.

Marika thought for just a tick and replied: "No."

"Ha! She gets it," the two giggled identically. Cian smiled and nodded his approval, too.

Then the two ran away – their legs tangling, their twin bodies falling head over foot with each other – and laughing all the harder for it as they went.

"Counting you, that makes ten," Marika announced to Cian.

"Ten what?" he responded, as he carefully chose a new stem of grass to chew on.

"Ten Fairies that I know for sure by their names: There's Wee Ann, Aisling the dreamer, Whip, Shifter, Yum, Fixer, and now Thackeray and Nan and Bob," she counted out on her fingers. "And you make ten."

"Mmmm," he expressed rather unimpressed.

"Why aren't the others letting me know them?" she asked.

"Give them time, Luv. You've only just arrived. And they let you *see* them, that's something. Most never meet even one of us in their lifetime, you know. What a greedy girl you are!"

"Sorry. I just was wondering."

But Cian was right. All the other Fairies did let Marika see them, named or not. And, most particularly, this happened when she sang. They would appear as if from thin air then, peeking over the banks of the pond or out from the depths of a hollow log or from behind the trunk of a fat old cypress tree or climbing up through the upturned roots of a fallen pine.

On the evening of a day somewhere in the third week (time was becoming somewhat irrelevant), Marika was singing a singularly lovely melody – when she was suddenly interrupted. This was a highly unique occurrence. Typically, no one would dream of disturbing the serenity and beauty of Marika singing. Cian, who was resting on one elbow, spellbound, balanced across two lily pads, splashed furiously into the water. Then, he saw who it was racing through the forest toward them.

It was Saoirse – a Fairy not yet introduced to Marika, but one of notable credibility and respect in the Fairy gathering.

"What is it?" Cian demanded as soon as Saoirse was within hearing.

"The man – the Traveller – Jacko," she replied breathlessly. "He's riding too near. He's heard her singing."

"Marika, come with me," Cian commanded the startled girl. He took her by the hand and pulled her toward an opening at the base of a fallen tree.

"But I won't fit..." she began to object.

Then Cian held tightly to her right arm, and Saoirse grabbed hold of the left. And she slipped easily underground with them.

The earth smelled damp and rich. Even in the semi-darkness, Marika could make out long passages and rooms with intricately carved chairs and sturdy tables and masterful drawings on the walls. She caught the slight aroma of freshly harvested fruits and berries and grasses.

All this passed over her as flashing impressions. Her main focus was to watch from the deep shadows, looking through a tangle of tree roots at the ground just above and in front of them. Within seconds, a horse came into view. On his back was a rider Marika had only seen once, but had never forgotten. Jacko.

He was large framed, strongly built. His thick, long, red hair was pulled back into a band at the base of his neck and hung in a mass down his broad back. He was terribly handsome. It made Marika feel uncomfortable to look at him. He was, as Wee Ann had so succinctly said, "cruel." She could smell it on him. See it in the eyes of the horse he rode. Sense it in the hard hands he used to pull the reins in too tightly.

Then, Marika noticed something that made her heart grow cold and hard as a stone against him. Around his throat he wore a long, deep green colored scarf. She knew that scarf. It belonged to Da. It was made of the finest silk, strong yet supple and the color of thick summer grass. Her mother had given it to Da before Marika was born. She had made it herself, he had told her. He never, ever, took it off. And yet, here it was – unmistakably there in front of her. Unmistakably and unbearably being worn around the thick, dirty neck of Jacko.

"Jacko," she spat his name out before Cian could press his hand over her mouth. She struggled free, but remembered discretion.

Jacko was listening to the wind. His eyes were scanning the woods, tree by tree. Rock by rock. He knew she was near. But the sun was setting. Twilight was deepening.

Then, quite faintly at first, overhead, the haunting sounds began. Stronger and louder they grew. Hollow wood clanging against wood in rhythmic chants; owls calling in secret messages; spirits whispering, whispering – first in Irish, then in English:

"Sean .... Sean ..... Sean .... Jacko ..... Jacko .... run .... RUN! ...."

Then, a loud "crack"! Something unseen stung the horse's rump, and the animal reared, its rider barely able to hold on.

Marika's mouth opened wide, she looked over at Cian. Only his eyes glinted in the darkness – like moonlight reflected off of deep water.

With a jerk on his horse's head, and a dig of his boot heels, Jacko turned and rode – with the speed and urgency of one whose very soul is being chased by ghosts – out of their presence, out of the forest. Only at the very edge of the enchanted woods did he stop, and turn, and curse silently, before he disappeared.

The three came up from their place of hiding.

"How do I thank you, Cian?" Marika spoke first. "... thank you both," she turned to Saoirse. "I am in debt to a stranger."

"My name is Saoirse," she said. "It means..."

"... *freedom*," Marika finished.

"God Bless you all for your friendship and magic," she called up into the trees around her. A flurry of wind that rustled the leaves and swayed the branches was her reply.

She looked back down as Cian and Saoirse were just leaving her. "And now, there are *eleven*," Cian called back to her with a sly smile and quiet splash as he returned to the water.

Sleep did not come for Marika that night. *Da's scarf ... Da's scarf ... Da's scarf ...* repeated and filled her head and soul with an impossible ache.

As the sun rose the following day, there was a grand gathering of the Fairies in the very center of the Carolina Bay. Marika expressed her appreciation to them again for hiding her and for turning Jacko away the night before.

And then, she told all of them about the scarf, her voice breaking and throbbing in fear and anger. "Your magic is strong," she said. "Can I be calling upon it to help me find what I seek?"

Not one of the Fairies hesitated to pledge all their abilities and loyalty to her quest.

Then she asked, "And may I be living among you until that time?" Her voice was not quite as steady as she had hoped. This was too important. And too possibly denied, she knew. A rare privilege being requested.

The Fairies' eyes all met, their heads nodded assent one to the next. They had become quite fond of this girl. But they understood the seriousness ... the consequence ... the ultimate requirement.

Without a word spoken, the Fairies all drew near and formed a circle about her. Clasping hands, they called on the spirits of the forest – the trees and grasses and brambles and bushes and all the living things there; the water, the mosses, the flowers, the birds in the air and the creatures that crept below; they called on the rocks and the very earth itself. Then they lifted up their hands and held fast to the wind and caught the sun and shadows – and, for one glittering, breathless moment, all stood still in time.

Cian, who remained apart from the circle, stepped in closely to Marika. He put his lips very near to her ear, whispering into it. It sounded like wind heard through pine branches just before a storm. And yet, the words were there, too: "For one year, Marika. You will have one year from now to decide. All four seasons you may stay and live among us. Then, you must leave and never return to this place – never even *speak* of this place. *Never remember!*" His breath barely brushed against her cheek as the words became even fainter. "But, if at the end of the year, you decide to stay ... you will remain here, unseen, *forever*. Do you understand?" His voice was barely audible. *"Will ... you ... abide?"*

Marika had wrapped her arms tightly around herself throughout the pronouncement, in part to keep her body still from the shivering that ran up and down it. She nodded and gave her solemn pledge.

"Then, it shall be," Cian said. He stepped away suddenly, quickly. At arm's length, he grasped Marika by both of her shoulders and looked deeply into her eyes. And he winked and laughed.

Marika's heart was beating so hard it thudded against her chest and in her ears. And yet, it felt as light as the very air.

*"**Go raibh maith agaibh,**"* she said to all around her. "Thank you."

SECRETS.

Summer crept into the Carolina Bay on the new wings of fledgling birds and emerging butterflies, and on the throaty trills of young frogs and the hissing of reborn cicadas.

Marika discovered that, like most of God's creatures and the natural world, Fairies are also drawn into the open more readily in summer than during any other season. Yet so adept are they at mimicry and deception that even she often found it difficult to differentiate them from authentic fireflies, or wildflowers dancing in an afternoon breeze, or morning sunlight glinting off pools of fresh clean rainwater.

Lying on her back at night, Marika would try to name the stars, brilliant in their black velvety robes. And she would excitedly point out to Cian – who was typically at her side – a shower of shimmering shooting stars, only to have him laugh heartily at her as the bright orbs alighted gently in the tops of the trees over their heads.

Marika spent long, hot afternoons lazily swimming in the coolness of the Bay and playing with all the Water Babies living there. Or she would nap in the deep, soft shade of a tall, citrus-scented magnolia tree.

In the evenings, she sang for her new friends, and they told each other amazing tales. They danced and laughed and performed elaborate skits and magic tricks and grew to trust each other.

In the mornings – while the cool breezes still drifted through the branches of the forest, and then down the sandy dirt roads of the town – Marika would cautiously walk into civilization, through the back streets and alleys, in early dawn shadows, before the town fully awoke. Here, she would find dropped coins or carelessly unlatched doors. Sometimes a shirt was left out on a clothesline. Sometimes a freshly baked pie or loaf of bread was forgotten on the sill of a window. A jug of milk was left to cool in a springhouse. Once, a stick of red and white candy wrapped in a kerchief was abandoned on the stump of a tree near a swing made of rope.

Marika was careful to repay these finds as best she could. A porch would be swept. Water might be drawn from the well. A lost toy would be put in plain view on a doorstep. Laundry would be taken from the line and neatly folded into a waiting basket. Fruits and vegetables were picked and placed by the door. Eggs were gathered. Perhaps less one or two samples, of course. But the service was done, nonetheless. And all without disturbing a soul.

That summer, the town would admit that there seemed to be more of the odd missing items – as well as an abundance of chores completed mysteriously – than was typically seen and noted. But there was no explanation. Maggie Nydegger had her suspicions, and kept them to herself. Joseph knew for certain, and kept equally silent. And the children, without exception, believed that the Fairies were behind it all. And the children, without exception, were not believed.

At least once a week, Marika visited Danny at his grave. She always brought him a treat and left it nestled in the dirt that was still achingly new yet slowly becoming flatter and firmer over rain-washed and sun-baked time: She gave him grass whistles and daisy-chains; smooth pebbles with remarkable colors or shapes, or sized perfectly for skipping across a pond; a magnificent blue marble she had found one early morning; a clever little boat that Cian had crafted for him from magnolia leaves and new green twigs; an abandoned butterfly wing.

One day, she discovered a small, beautifully carved, wooden likeness of a pony tucked near the headstone that now marked his gravesite. It was not something she had brought to him. But it was a treat he would have adored. It made her think of Joseph, somehow. Marika missed Joseph terribly, even though her days were filled with the society of Fairies. She never forgot Joseph's kindness. She thought often and sadly of Maggie, as well. But her heart was still far from forgiving.

Marika knew Joseph had tried to come see her many times over the weeks and months that had passed since he had led her to the threshold of the forest and the Carolina Bay. But he had been unable to find her. This was due in no small part to the actions of Marika herself.

In the days following Jacko's visit to the forest in search of Marika – when he had come terrifyingly close to finding her – Marika had used some of the skills Gran had developed in her to conceal and guard. She had carefully defined the edges of the enchanted center of the forest, and there she created marks of protection – ancient signs of a people from long ago and another land. She carved these signs on trees, etched them on rocks, engraved them in the very earth itself. A cadre of Fairies worked at her side, adding their own magic and strengthening hers. Their spells were not dissimilar – even the language each used had familiar sounds, one with the other.

The effect was a mystical veil of secrecy that caused humans – whether actual seekers or casual passersby – to be unable to see or pass through this curtain of protection. Regardless of how close one came – even to the very gates of the entrance itself – the spells held the intruder at bay, often confused, blinded to all that was kept and guarded behind it.

Sounds, however, could penetrate and carry from one world to the next, both in and out. The Fairies used their magic here, as well. With haunting winds, and chimes seemingly coming from nowhere and everywhere, wood that knocked with the echo of old bones, ghostly whispers that chanted the names of powerful spirits – most visitors took leave with haste and weren't soon to return.

Only one came with regularity and called out to Marika herself. He called her "Colleen." And he called her "Child." He never spoke her secret name. And when Marika would hear Joseph's voice, asking for her, calling for her, she would stop and listen and was strongly tempted to go to him, to let him see her. It was only out of respect for her oath and the Fairies that she kept herself hidden and silent.

One morning, however, she awoke from a deep sleep and a dark dream she could not quite remember. She was filled with unease. Her back burned as if it had been stung a thousand times by Whip's unseen weapons. Her arms ached. And she felt a terrible dread in her heart.

She immediately sat up and rubbed her arms and reached to feel her back. All seemed normal. And then she saw, sitting just a few feet away from her, the Fairy known as Aisling, the dream or vision Fairy.

Aisling was crouched low, bent double. Her eyes were hollow and devoid of light. She was rocking from side to side, moaning with an unearthly sound. It sickened Marika's soul.

"Aisling," Marika called out, "tell me the dream."

"It is not a dream," the Fairy responded in lifeless tones.

"Tell me the vision," Marika persisted.

"Beaten. A black man is beaten ... bleeding. His blood is red. His blood is alive. But his spirit is dead. It has been tortured out of him," Aisling chanted with agony, barely audible.

"Is he a slave?" Marika asked.

Marika knew of slavery, of course. But very little first-hand. In Boston, as a child and a gypsy, she had been removed from the practice as well as the politics of it. Slavery had been outlawed in Massachusetts for more than a generation. And her *thribli* were simply not involved with it in any state. They lived "outside," a separate society.

Once, however, when she was quite young, Marika's Da had lifted her on his shoulders during a day at the market in downtown Boston. They were stopped to hear a man speaking in the public square. Marika remembered only bits and pieces of what the man had said – but he had spoken eloquently, passionately, about the horrors and injustice of slavery and how morally insane it was. Even her child's ear and comprehension caught the underlying message. And, ever after, she had felt somehow ashamed that the country in which she lived would tolerate such sin and cruelty anywhere within its borders.

"He is a man of dark color," Aisling was moaning again.

"A *slave*?" Marika repeated.

"The man who is beaten ... the man who is beating him ... both are black men," Aisling replied. "He is his *brother* ... he is his *master*."

Aisling rocked and groaned, rocked and groaned, and then faded away into the rising sun.

Marika shivered. She was unable to make sense of the Fairy's words or vision. She felt cold everywhere inside, although her skin was slick with perspiration. She stood up on unsteady legs. And then she heard the voice – Joseph was calling her. This time, she knew she would answer.

Marika slipped through the gates of the veil just as Joseph, on horseback, was heading away, out of the forest.

"Joseph," she spoke quietly.

He turned toward her with an expression of immense relief, followed by great and genuine joy at seeing his small friend again.

"Child," he began, as he dismounted the horse. "Thank you for coming. Why have you stayed hidden so long – from me?"

Marika's heart, too, was overjoyed at seeing this man who had meant so much to her in such a brief time. *"Old souls,"* her Gran would have named them.

"Oh, Joseph," Marika called again – this time with open arms and running feet. She embraced him with more happiness and longing than she realized she had ready to release at seeing him again.

They sat together on a fallen log and ate oranges that Joseph had brought with him. The horse was grazing contentedly nearby. They talked of Maggie first.

"She misses you very much," Joseph said quietly, watching her face.

Marika nodded silently.

"She feels terribly sorry for letting you down. She knows how hurt you must have felt – how angry you were," Joseph continued.

Marika spit out a seed.

"She's started teaching again," he said looking down at the section of orange he was pulling from the body of the fruit.

Marika watched him with admitted interest. "Teaching?"

"Mmm. She does it at night – in secret." Joseph knew the girl would be more intrigued than sullen.

"Why?"

"Because her students are slaves," he answered simply.

Even in her relative ignorance, Marika knew this was against the law – at least in the South.

"Why does she do it?" the girl asked.

"Because Maggie never could obey a rule she thinks is wrong," he replied. "And she knows these people are going to need to be able to read and write to ever have a chance at freedom."

"What would happen if she got caught?" Marika asked after a bit.

"Nothin' good, that's for sure. The law can be harsh, even for a woman," he replied. "And even worse for the slaves themselves," he added.

"But she's being careful, right?" Marika worried in spite of herself.

"Well, she's been caught at it before. But I think she's taking extra precautions this time," Joseph said, perhaps more reassuringly than he felt.

"Are you a slave, Joseph?" Marika asked plainly.

"No. I was granted my freedom twenty-nine years ago last month," Joseph replied with exactitude. "My mother and father were born slaves in Charleston – plantation slaves. But Doc Jackson's father – he was a doctor too, old Doc Rufus Jackson – bought my mother and daddy as house slaves when he got married and set up housekeeping and opened his medical office here in town. They moved up from the low country right around 1805 or so, I believe. Well, old Doc Rufus got real fond of both of them – so did his wife, Miss Lucy," Joseph paused then to offer the last slice of his orange to Marika and scatter the peelings out to the gathering birds and squirrels.

Marika was enjoying hearing Joseph's story. Her mouth was full of juice, but she swallowed a few times, wiped her lips and hands with the hem of her skirt, and asked Joseph to tell her more.

Joseph tried to offer Marika his handkerchief, but her skirt served the purpose before he could get it out of his pocket. He dried his own fingers and mouth, returned the kerchief to his back pocket, rested his elbows on his knees, and continued his story for the young listener.

"Well, like I said, my mamma and daddy were born slaves – so was their folks, and their folks before them. In fact, my family traces back to before most of the white folks around here. But Doc Rufus was a righteous man. He didn't much hold a good thought for slavery. But it was the only way he knew. So, when old Doc Rufus got married, he bought daddy and mamma and brought 'em up here to keep house for him and Miss Lucy. Do you know, I was born on the very same day that Miss Lucy gave birth to her son, Walt. The very same day. But Miss Lucy ... she wasn't very strong, and she died before Walt was even a week old. So my mamma nursed him and raised him and loved him just like she loved me. Yessir. She loved him with a true mother's heart. It was like we were true, natural brothers."

Joseph paused, but Marika was captivated and listened intently.

Joseph continued: "Well, old Doc Rufus never remarried the rest of his life. And on his deathbed – twenty-nine years and one month ago – he granted me and my mamma our freedom. My daddy had passed a few years before that. Then mamma died not long after."

Joseph seemed to be done talking, so Marika raised some questions of her own: "So why didn't you leave? Why do you stay working for Doc? And why don't you call him by his Christian name when that's how he speaks to you?"

Joseph looked Marika square in the face and said: "Walt Jackson is one of the finest men I know – white or black. He's been my best friend – my brother – all our lives. I've got a good life here. I know just about as much medicine and doctoring as he does, too. He taught me everything he learned all through school. Still keeps me reading and learning all the things that other doctors are finding out. He's a good man."

He continued then, almost as if Marika hadn't been present. A cloud temporarily covered the sun and darkened Joseph's face as well. A breeze picked up and scattered bits of leaves and bark and swirled them about uneasily.

"I was there when Walt met the woman he would love all his life," he remembered. "I shared his joy as if it was me falling head-over-heels for the most beautiful woman alive. And I was there when she brought the twins into this world – a boy and a girl – Jacob and Jenny. Such happy, good babies they were. And I was there when we got the news of the carriage accident that took them all away from us. So sudden – so cruel. Like a dream it was. I thought Doc would never recover from it. But I was there when he laid them all to rest – one little one on either side of her. I sat with him. Made him eat. Kept him from drinking himself to death. And I was there when he brought himself back to life – to save another child in a carriage accident. Another child lived that day because of my friend. And if I choose to call him Doc and say 'yessir' and 'no sir' and he chooses to call me Joseph, then that's just the way it is."

Joseph looked at Marika with eyes too wise for doubt. "Why would I leave my friend now?"

Marika nodded in understanding.

The two shared several minutes of silence. Then Marika's earlier experience with Aisling the dream Fairy came hauntingly back to her. She hesitated to tell Joseph about the Fairies or Aisling herself, so she tried to search out the interpretation on her own.

"Joseph," she began, "when you were a slave, were you ever beaten – with a whip, I mean?"

"Beaten, yes. When I was about ten or eleven, a neighbor of Doc

Rufus accused me of stealing his horse. He had me bound to a fence and beat me soundly. But not with a whip. He used a flat paddle, because a paddle doesn't leave the lash marks of a whip, so the beating can be denied if necessary. The paddle is still used mostly on slaves who will be traded later – it keeps them unmarked and doesn't give evidence of them having a problem with obedience." Joseph's face had become quite hard. His words were spoken plainly, but bitterly.

Marika continued her questions, however. "*Were* you stealing that horse?"

"Yes."

"Why?"

"Because the man was thoroughly abusing it – with whips and branches and stones. It was cruelty I couldn't bear to watch," Joseph confessed.

"What happened after the man caught you and beat you?" Marika pursued.

"Doc Rufus tended to my back, bought the horse, and we never encountered that man or spoke of it again. I believe there was more to it than that – but nothing I was privileged to know."

"Can I see your back where you were beaten?" Marika asked.

"No."

"Was the man who hit you a black man?" she questioned, thinking of the Aisling dream.

"No, Child, he was a white man. Why are you asking me such questions?" he wanted to know.

But Marika thought it best to leave her disclosure of the Fairies to a later time. She changed the subject abruptly.

"Where were you going today?" she asked. "And why do you have Doc's bag with you?" she pointed to the medical bag Joseph had attached to his horse's saddle.

"I told you I know doctoring pretty good. And sometimes Doc Jackson sends me to attend to someone if he can't get there himself. That is, when it's a slave or another black person," Joseph clarified. "White folks don't much take to a black doctor. I've just been to see a man who works for one of the potters here in the woods. A broken ankle. I bound it and was on my way back when I thought I'd try calling for you again. I call for you whenever I'm in the woods. But, this time, you came," he smiled.

"Yes. This time I came."

"Do you hear me those other times?" he asked.

"Yes."

"Why do you stay away? I know you come into town sometimes, too. Why don't you let me see you?" Joseph asked with genuine concern.

"I've promised," she tried to answer.

"Promised who?"

"Some new friends," she struggled to find words that would satisfy without revealing.

"Are you living among the spirits of the forest – the Fairies of the Carolina Bay?" Joseph prodded suddenly with a sly smile.

Marika was silent.

"So you are, then," Joseph nodded. "I just knew there was the 'mystic' about you. I thought you would be at home there," he said with self-satisfaction and a single loud clap of his hands. "The gypsy girl and the Fairies," he threw his head back and laughed.

"Are you happy?" he suddenly put forth quite seriously.

She was unable to contain her smile. "Oh yes, Joseph, yes! Happier than I've been in such a long time. Except ..."

"Except what?" he asked.

"Nothing. I'm very happy," she pushed the experience with Jacko away from the moment.

They rose together then and began walking along the banks of the wide creek that ran through the middle of the forest. Joseph led the horse, and Marika decided to tell her friend about her encounters with the Fairies. She described some of them and their antics in detail to his complete delight. She also explained about the guardian veil in the forest and how it protected them all. But, for reasons known only to her own heart, she held back from him the pledge she had made to the Fairies in exchange for the privilege of living among them.

While they walked, the two friends passed near the potteries that actively thrived along the water's edges. Many slaves participated in the manufacturing of the valued wares. Some were highly skilled artisans. As they passed, Joseph spoke to a few of the workers by name, both black and white. Marika kept to the shadows and was noticed only peripherally.

Occasionally, Marika would stoop and pick up a shard of discarded broken pottery. She would study each piece carefully for a moment, and then slip the more delicate, beautiful bits into her pocket, and toss the less attractive ones back into the mud.

Subtly, Marika guided their path toward Danny's grave. When they reached the cemetery gates, they both looked carefully down the many pathways to assure their privacy. Marika still crept from tree to tree, headstone to monument, until she felt safe enough to sit openly at the edge of the gravesite where her beloved brother slept in peace.

She lay on her stomach and neatly placed the pottery shards on top of the grave in intricate, meaningful designs. She made a cross and a flower with many petals and a crescent moon. Then she plucked away any dried leaves or dead blossoms or stray branches.

"Did you bring Danny this?" she pointed to the carved wooden pony.

"Yes," Joseph answered.

"Thank you. He would have loved it. He would have loved you," she said shyly.

"I'm sorry I never knew him," Joseph said.

Then he said, "Do you know where I got that pony?" as he watched her closely.

"Didn't you make it?" she asked.

"No. Actually, it was carved by Maggie's husband. He made it for their youngest son before he died. She saved it all these years. And then she gave it to me to bring to Danny's grave."

Marika was silent; her throat too tight to speak.

"I'll tell her thank you for you," Joseph said.

She nodded.

But before either could say another word, Marika darted off behind a large nearby headstone, just as a young black child came running toward them.

"Mista Joseph, Mista Joseph ... you gotta come quick," he said breathlessly. "He done kilt him fo' sure dis time. Kilt him dead fo' sure!" The young boy was nearly hysterical.

Joseph grabbed him by the shoulders and shook him gently. "Calm down, now, get your breath, Caleb. I'll come with you. Who is it? Where is he?" He threw a quick glance toward Marika's hiding place as he was lifting the boy onto the back of his horse. He had stepped into the saddle himself, pulling the boy up behind him.

Marika heard the child say: "It's Ishmael, Mista Joseph ... he done been brought back. Massah's got him down at the cabins now."

Joseph rode down the lane and out of the graveyard. At the gates, he turned the horse to the left, away from town. He looked back again for Marika, but she was nowhere to be found.

Following Joseph and Caleb was not difficult for Marika, even though they were on horseback. She kept them in view for most of the way, and picked up their trail easily the few times she lost sight of them.

Not far along, they turned into a long, central driveway leading to a gracious old plantation house. The dirt-packed road was straight but jagged-edged, thick on both sides with gardenia bushes that filled the air with Southern summer scent. Despite the glorious fragrance, the blossoms were past their white pristine beauty, now clinging in curled yellow-brown decadence to their still rich green leaves.

Marika crossed behind the wide bushes, over cool green ivy that lay as an ankle-deep carpet beneath full low magnolia trees. These tree-borne flowers, too, had aged beyond their peak of loveliness. Many of the huge blossoms were now strewn over the ground, broken and dying and unheeded.

Joseph and his passenger had ridden past the house, its white paint peeling in the humid heat, mimicking the scorched dying flower petals that surrounded it. They continued down a rough, worn dirt path, then crossed brown lawns under drooping tree limbs with sweeping curtains of Spanish Moss, past curling grape vines and gardens of ripening vegetables, right to the very edge of a swiftly moving stream.

Here, Joseph reached behind him, grabbed Caleb by the forearm, and swung him down to the ground; the boy's bare feet raised thick red dust from the soft soil as he ran into the nearest cabin. Joseph lifted himself down as well, releasing his medical bag, handing his reins to the nearest waiting child, following the boy through an open doorway.

Marika walked forward quietly. Her curiosity and concern temporarily brought her out of her self-imposed hiding. The handful of people sitting and standing on rotting front steps and in chicken-scratched yards watched her with wide silent looks, but no one questioned her presence. They were, for the most part, very old or very young, and all people of color.

"Hello," she spoke to the child holding Joseph's horse.

"Miss," was the reply.

The chickens made the only sounds in the surrounding hush. Even the breeze held its breath as she walked by the residents, and noted the world that enclosed them. Meager clothing was drying on a makeshift line; some bits of material were also lying on the stream bank rocks, wet and steaming in the summer sun. Small patches of vegetables struggled near the cabin doors. A thin yellow dog scratched his fleas while his eyes tracked the approaching girl carefully. The smell of pork fat and onions and collards reeked through the open doorways and clung to the bare wooden walls of the weary, leaning cabins. Each impossibly small house was identical to the next. Marika counted four. A few toddlers stood on unsure legs, naked from the waist down; tattered shirts covered their tiny shoulders and backs and chests. Marika envisioned those same innocent bodies welted and bleeding and she blinked and breathed in hard to push the images away.

As she reached the door of the cabin into which Joseph and Caleb had disappeared, she heard the sounds of suppressed pain and anger. Joseph's was the angriest.

She looked into the darkness, her eyes slowly adjusting. A single chair and small table were in the center of a room that seemed to be the entire house. To her left, Joseph was kneeling next to a narrow rope bed. It was a tangle of old, stained sheets, which she soon discerned included the body of a man. The lump of bedding writhed in pain every time Joseph touched his hand to it. Soon, she could see the man – his back was covered in wounds, some were bleeding, some were scar tissue. Very little of his skin was left untouched. He smelled of sweat and blood and urine. Joseph was cleaning the new cuts and applying an ointment as gently as he could. But his slightest touch seemed to burn the beaten man afresh.

The man then began to weep. And this cut more deeply into Marika's heart and mind than the physically torn flesh laid out in front of her. She had slipped silently near to Joseph's shoulder. She reached out her hand and stroked the weeping man's head. He quieted at her touch, but his tears still ran with bitterness.

"Did Isaac do this, Ishmael?" Joseph asked the man with a hard deepness to his voice.

"He said it should be done," was the man's responding cry.

"Your own brother would have this done to you?" Joseph was shaking with anger. He stopped to steady his hand before laying a clean bandage across the wounds.

The tortured man cried out more bitterly then. "M' back has felt da whip and da rod before. But he is my brother! He suppos' to buy and pay for us to keep us safe. He beats mo' dan m' back. He beats m' soul."

"I thought he had sent you away," Joseph said. "I thought you were up North."

"He say Ishmael run away!" This time, a woman spoke from the shadows in a corner of the room. "He pays money to gets him back, and den he done beats him like a white man. He no better dan dat!" And she began to cry as well.

Joseph finished his treatment with tenderness and silence.

Marika began to croon softly as she stroked her hand across the beaten man's head and he fell under her spell. All in the room did. Peace, at least for the moment, filled their hearts.

Joseph packed up his bag and walked out of the door. The woman from the shadows followed him. "Keep the wounds clean, and use this ointment until they heal," he told her. "And send Caleb for me if he gets worse."

"It ain't his back dat is torn and bleedin' so much as his heart," she said. "He trusted Isaac. Loved him. Why dat man do such a ting?"

But there was no answer. No comfort Joseph could offer. He mounted his waiting horse and, this time, reached down for Marika's hand; he pulled her up behind him and they rode away from the cabins in silence.

They didn't go far. When they reached the front of the big house, Marika saw a black man – well dressed and overly fed – standing among a string of horses. He was obviously dealing for their purchase.

Marika could tell the animals were fit and healthy, but she also detected a tension running through the line. They all watched with rolling eyes and flattened ears as the trader who was selling them came near – a white man, wearing a large-brimmed dark hat.

Joseph pulled his horse up and passed the reins to Marika as he swung his right leg across the horse's neck in front of him and slipped quickly to the ground.

"Isaac ... Isaac Winston! I will talk to you, Sir. Now!" he called with authority.

The black man dropped the horse's hoof he was holding between his knees while he examined it and turned with indignation toward the man who had dared to interrupt his business dealings. When he recognized Joseph, he relaxed a bit, waving him over to the side of the house, away from the horse trader. Marika could no longer hear the words, but their postures and faces communicated the exchange clearly.

Marika's focus wandered from the arguing men back to the string of horses just in time to see the back of the horse trader's head as he turned and stooped to hide himself behind one of the animals. His hat was in his hand. His hair was long and red, gathered in a band at the base of his neck. And, around that neck there flowed a dark green silk scarf.

Marika found she couldn't breathe properly; the air and light around her became unnatural, unreal. Joseph had returned and remounted the horse in front of her. But his own anger and outrage blinded his eyes to her obvious distress.

Joseph urged the horse away with such force that Marika barely had time to instinctively grab on to his coat to keep from falling. She could feel the anger and tension across Joseph's back like boulders beneath the quiet surface of a forest pond.

"Joseph," she began.

"No," he bit back. "Not now, Child. Not now."

He took her to the edge of where he had found her earlier that day. Neither had spoken a word. She slid to the ground. And, unexpectedly, Joseph followed. He led the horse to grass and sat himself on a nearby tree stump. He motioned for her to sit next to him.

When she had crouched herself into a small bundle on the grass beside him, he put his head in his hands and rubbed his close-cropped thinning hair.

"Slavery is evil, Child," he began with a husky voice. "Pure evil. No man should be allowed to hold such feelings in his chest. His mind should never conceive of it. His heart should never experience it. It is the very devil inside us – and it leaves sorely little room for God."

"Are you speaking of the slave owner or the slave?" Marika questioned.

Joseph pulled his hands away from his face and looked at her for a long time as she absently picked at strands of grass and wild flowers and shredded them in her fingers, letting them fall back to the ground.

"Both, I suppose," he responded at last. "Both."

And then he continued almost to himself. "But, Child, it is never so shameful – so purely evil – as when both are people of color. When both are blood brothers!" This last died away in a choke of his voice.

"Aisling saw it," Marika commented quietly with remembrance and sudden understanding.

"Who is Aisling?" Joseph asked in confusion and curiosity.

"She is a dream."

And then Marika told Joseph about Jacko. She spoke of her intended marriage to him, but her desire to hide instead. She revealed in detail about his coming into the forest, almost finding her. She described Da's scarf, and her suspicions about Jacko's possession of it. And, finally, she disclosed to Joseph about seeing Jacko not more than an hour earlier at the plantation. By the time she had finished, her words were mere whispers, and she trembled with fear and rage.

Joseph just kept shaking his head in deep sympathy and overwhelmed concern.

"Come into town, Child," he pleaded. "Let us protect you, help you."

"I'm safer here," she insisted. And he could not argue.

Marika stood and put a hand on each of Joseph's shoulders. She kissed him tenderly on both cheeks. She stepped back and said: "My name is Marika. Call me with this name when you need to see me." Then, within ten steps, she was gone.

Neither she nor Joseph saw the murky, motionless, shadow

watching from just a few yards away. Only the late afternoon sun flitted across a bit of green silk.

THE DOG.

For four days and nights rain had been steadily sliding over slick magnolia leaves and dripping down long–needled pines in a constant rhythm that hissed and tapped and plopped into swirling puddles on shining soaked earth.

The sky remained the color of steel, with clouds curling across it edged in purple and black. Thunder would at times add deep baritone comments. But no lightning relieved the sameness of the gray daylight hours.

The Carolina Bay was rising perceptibly. And Marika's peninsula was receding at an alarming rate. She had created an effective slanted roof – a sort of half-hut-like structure – with pine boughs and leaves. But even with that protection, she was being forced to consider the possibility of moving underground, as she was frequently urged to do by the Fairies. The freedom and familiarity of the above-ground forest, however, was too compelling for her, even as she now determined the need to relocate – at the very least, a bit more inland.

Autumn had cooled the soft summer days into early sunsets and shortened shadows. The mornings were a medley of gray mists and white fogs and sparkling silver dews.

Marika marveled at how the forest maintained its shades of

brilliant greens in this southern environment – long after the frost would have nipped her northern trees into brassy golds and fiery reds, and then soon stripped them to their barky bones. She also adored still napping in the warm afternoon sun, or swimming in the coolness of the Bay, and watching thick moist hazes encircle the evening moon. She was, quite happily, relearning all she knew to be true about late October and early November.

A few weeks before these recent, unrelenting rains had begun, arriving gaggles of geese had surprised the solemnity and stillness of the Bay with noisy bluster. They poked into the long, fragrant grasses and winding inlets, and called unceasingly to one another with hoarse, throaty exclamations and complete disregard for the hour or sleepiness of their native neighbors. Like Marika, the geese, too, seemed utterly enthralled with finding such plentiful warmth and nourishment at such a late time of the year.

Cian and the other Water Fairies were the most disturbed by it all. They grumbled and cursed and made unkind remarks and did their best to cope or at least stay out of the paths of the temporary intruders. Most of the time.

But one particularly warm and inviting day, when the geese were especially ill behaved, Cian impulsively leaped onto the back of the largest gander in the pond. He grabbed the remnants of a nearby cattail reed, yanked it loose, and began smacking the goose soundly on its head and tail in the most irritating way. The offended bird tried to rise into the air, but Cian's unexpected weight and his unrelenting grasp on its wings kept the gander close to the water's surface. Within minutes, other Water Fairies had joined in the game. And before Marika knew what was happening, races were inevitably underway from one side of the pond to the other.

The geese were quick to enjoy themselves as well, once the sense of alarm had subsided and the spirit of fun took hold. Geese, Marika learned, are typically a serious lot. But after being brought into the game, they became quite committed and surprisingly sportsman-like.

Within half-a-dozen races, wagering began among the other Fairies, of course, and cheers arose as battles were closely run, often won by the merest width of a feather. The games lasted for a full day and a half. But then, the gray skies slid in, the rains commenced, and the geese moved on to their next port-of-call. And things settled down into a daily, drizzly, routine.

Marika had located a patch of high ground not far from her peninsula where she had decided to construct her new lean-to. She had just begun to break and gather branches of pine for materials when the Fairy known as Fixer joined her. Soon, others assembled as well. Fairies can rarely resist becoming involved when it comes to building projects. Being an inherited trait and inborn ability from ages ago, they are typically brilliant at it – if only a bit bossy. Marika was soon dismissed to go gather a particular type of vine that would be used to finish securing the branches together perfectly, while the Fairies themselves set about the actual building of the structure.

Marika did as she was told. She happily dodged beneath the trees, keeping out of the steady thumping of rain as much as possible, gathering the vines she sought as she went. She wound them carefully round and round, over the top of her left shoulder and thumb, then under the crook of her elbow, making a neat coil as she went.

About a mile out into the forest, she reached one particularly massive tangle of the vine and began pushing and pulling at it to break it loose. A pitiful, mournful "yelp" came from the very center of the mass. Marika peered into the dark den created by the woven plant, and saw two bright and frightened eyes gleaming back at her.

A throaty warning growl followed. Then, silence.

"Hush now, Creature," Marika began to speak softly. "It's only a girl wanting a bit of vine."

The animal growled again and tried to lunge, but released a sad, high-pitched, soulful sound instead. Its pain and fear were obvious and heart-wrenching.

Marika let the load of vine she had gathered drop to the ground. She continued to talk and croon and whisper to the stranger. Then, as she slowly pulled some of the vines back, making a larger opening, she saw a dank, reddish-yellow dog hunched low in the mud and tangle of wood.

"A dog you are then," she observed quietly. "And where do you come from I wonder?"

She crouched her own body down as low as she could get, balled tightly, as small as she could become. She kept her eyes and face averted from the dog as much as possible. Slowly, she held out one hand, palm down, open wide. And she offered it to the dog to smell. The other arm she kept close in, wrapped around herself. All the while, she sang to the animal calmly. She turned her palm upward and moved her fingers slowly.

Within a few minutes, the dog's fear had abated, and Marika was stroking his ears and neck. But, as Marika tried to coax him out of his hiding place, he yelped with pain whenever he moved even a few inches.

Marika worked steadily, carefully, removing branch after branch, vine after vine, until she could see the dog and his trappings clearly. His right shoulder had become entwined with a large, ugly, thickly thorned plant that she did not recognize. It was vine-like with fat, moist, yet unyielding, tendrils. Hideously gray-green and black in color, it curled and twined and insinuated itself into everything it could touch. Between its large black thorns the size of claws, it had smaller thorny teeth and spines, so that it offered no clear place to grasp and unfurl it from whatever it clutched. About half way along its length, it had slashed the dog's flesh and become imbedded in it. With gentle hands and calming voice, Marika began her best efforts to free the tortured animal. Her own flesh caught and bled while she worked, but she was careful not to jerk away or move too abruptly, to not frighten the animal any more than he already was, and to not deepen the injury to his back and side. She was soaked to the skin from the rain, her hands punctured and sliced, when she was at last able to release the animal and examine his injury.

"Well, Dog, it's not so bad now," she said comfortingly. "We'll be making you well and fit again in no time. But you best be coming with me, so I can tend to you proper like." Marika spoke to the dog with great tenderness and respect. And the creature responded in kind. Listening to her every word, he limped along behind her as she picked up her own gathered vines in her weary hands and returned to the place where the hut was being built for her.

"Ho! Luv. What have you there hobbling behind you?" Cian called from the clearing as Marika and the dog stepped out of the foliage. He lowered the mud ball with which he was filling cracks in the hut and stooped to look over the dog.

"It's a dog I've found, and an injured one at that," Marika responded.

"Are you sure it's a dog?" Nan and Bob called in unison from the backside of the lean-to. "Could be a fox or a wolf. Could be something else," they said as they shook their heads and watched the creature come cautiously near.

"It's a dog," Marika assured them, shaking her own head at the way these two loved to cast doubt on even the most obvious of situations. "And he'll be needing our help. Caught his shoulder in a thorny mess," she motioned to the injury as she handed Fixer the coil of vine she had gathered. She knelt next to the dog and bade him to lie down with a mere movement of her hand.

"And look at you, too, Marika," scolded Fixer. "What did you have to do to free the creature? Fight off a demon?" He clucked his tongue over her hands and began wiping the blood clear with a handful of moist moss.

The rain had all but ceased by then, and more Fairies came out to inspect and greet the newcomer.

"What kind?" Wee Ann asked. "Pointy ears down. Curly tail up. Color like early morning," she observed as she circled the animal slowly. "Doesn't eat Fairies?" she asked Marika.

"Do you eat Fairies?" Marika in turn asked the dog with a smile.

The dog yawned widely. "He says to please not concern yourself over such matters at all. He has no taste for you," Marika interpreted. "Although he must be terribly hungry. His ribs are fairly poking through his skin," she continued thinking out loud as she ran her hands down his sides and legs, feeling carefully for more injuries or ailments.

"This leg has been broken in the past – but healed well, I believe," Fixer added as he also petted the dog gently and pressed against his left forepaw.

The animal's eyes never left Marika, but politely avoided direct eye contact with her. He scarcely noted the Fairies who surrounded him in gracious acceptance.

"He's not been around humans much," Marika concluded. "He only knows a dog's way of talking and listening," she relayed.

Wee Ann, who had disappeared for a few minutes returned then with her hands wound in spider webs. "For healing," she said as she began gently laying the gauzy cure across the dog's shoulder wound. "Make him good. Soon. You too," she handed some of the natural healer to Marika as well.

Marika thanked the tiny Fairy and gave her the things she had gathered on her trek back to help treat the wounds as well – wild honey for infection and willow bark for pain.

Many of the Fairies took part in the wound cleaning and tending for both the dog's shoulder and Marika's hands. Then the Fairy known as Thackeray went to gather food for her and her new-found friend. Marika was careful to not thank him. But she took the nourishment from him with a gentle smile and a grateful heart.

The dog ate its purposefully portioned meal from Marika with a strong appetite that she was glad to see. She knew she must build him up slowly, steadily. Then, with his hunger abated, his wound cleaned and dressed, and his pain minimized, he closed his eyes twice, and was deeply, exhaustedly, asleep at the girl's side.

She greatly admired the small hut her friends had completed for her. It was sturdy and rainproof and would withstand considerable wind. Yet it allowed her freedom to the open sky and breezes, to all the colors and fragrances, all the emotion and rhythms and music of the surrounding forest and Bay. A soft, pinestraw sleeping mat was thick and cozy within the most-protected corner of the hut. A rock-and-mud fire circle was positioned nearby. And, she noticed, carefully drawn symbols of protection surrounded her and her new home. She also noted with pleased reassurance that she was situated just a few yards away from tree-rooted access to some of the Fairies' own underground dwellings.

In appreciation, Marika sang especially meaningful and beautiful songs that evening – about home and family and the love of God for all His creatures. And the Fairies said their goodnights with warm hearts and tired hands from a long day's blessing of work for a friend.

The last drops of rain fell and dried in slow motion as a soft breeze drifted them away. The dog snuggled closer to Marika's knees. She stroked his tired head and wished him only happy dreams. Cian stretched himself out on the ground a few feet away. Together they watched the clouds break apart and silver moonbeams fill the forest, making it bright as day. Deep violet shadows danced under the trees. The water of the Bay glistened starlight back to the skies.

"Dog is a different kind of creature, isn't he?" Marika admitted to Cian after looking the animal over again in the light of the moon and the evening campfire.

"I've seen some a bit like him before," Cian observed. "Wild, they are. They don't take to living with people. I've seen them mostly just out on their own, roaming the forest, being and letting be."

Marika stroked the dog's pointed ears and noted how he kept them close to his head most of the time. Not out of fear or anger, but simply as the way he carried them.

"He could catch a fish with that tail," she laughingly pointed out to Cian. "Curled like a hook – but it's not been broken."

"And does he cover his droppings in sand – with his nose?" Cian then asked with sudden remembrance.

"Yes," Marika answered in surprise. "And his wetting as well."

"Well, then," Cian nodded, "he's a wild one for sure. They're the only ones to be doing that with their leavings. Not like most dogs, who scratch and kick and throw their scent about to be smelled and noted by all who come after them. These prefer to pass by unnoticed. Unseen," he concluded.

"How clever of you, Dog," Marika spoke to the soundly sleeping animal. "Whoever might be following after you would not trouble to seek you out – believing you'd passed by ages ago, with your droppings all covered with sand like that. And to be doing it with your nose makes for a job well done, I suspect."

"And will we be calling him 'Dog'?" Cian asked rightly, grinning at her.

"I have been thinking about that," Marika said.

"And you've decided..." Cian prompted.

"I believe I'll be calling him 'Conrí'," she announced.

"Ah, yes," Cian responded, "Irish for King of the Hounds. Very fitting, my dear. But please do fatten him up soon. It's a pity seeing a 'king' looking like a good puff of breeze might knock him off his feet." With that, Cian dove into the Bay and laughter filled the bubbles behind him.

The dog only snuggled tighter to his new companion without ever even opening an eye. He slept more solidly and less frightened than he had in many, many months. And little did he suspect that he was now a "king."

Marika's hand never left him the entire night.

Conrí watched and followed Marika throughout the whole of the next day and evening. His injury was already beginning to improve, and the pain had subsided significantly. His devotion to the girl was not only absolute, but against all of his natural instincts. Somewhere buried in the dog's ancestral memory was the wolf's life in the wilds of Asia; the experience of following primitive man across the Bering land-bridge; of eventually coming to settle in this southern place. Perhaps he knew in his blood that he was the last of his kind, unique now only to the Carolinas, especially well suited to a solitary life in the plentiful woodlands of the area. Somewhere he had learned to live only on the very outer edges of human society and consciousness, to take what the humans cast off, but with the simple act of opportunity – never a sense of gratitude or indebtedness or dependency.

Deep in Conrí's heart, he was unsure of his yearning to be with Marika. To be near her, watching her, hearing her voice, feeling her warmth, brought him great but unaccustomed comfort. Perhaps he would revert soon to his solitary, aloof ways. But, for the time being, he was drawn to her presence with an unexpected strength and peace.

A few days later (or perhaps it had been weeks, as time slid and folded over and under itself almost imperceptibly now) the morning broke with a brilliant, cloudless sunrise. The sky enriched into a blue so deep and clear, Marika thought she might be peeking into the floor of heaven itself.

All about her, the forest was beginning to crisp and shade into autumn scents and colors. The Bay reflected soft yellows and oranges at the edges of the trees. The earth smelled of rich brown molds from beneath layers of rain-soaked leaves that had warmed in pools of sunlight.

When she walked the back roads in and near town, she caught the aromas of freshly baked pies through open windows and wood smoke curling from cozy cottage chimneys. A faint, almost forgotten emptiness caught in her chest as she crept along the early morning edges of town. It was a hollow space, where once there had been Danny and Gran and Da and all those who had held her close and loved her. She couldn't remember the last time Joseph had called for her in the woods.

Marika found herself leaning behind a large oak tree at the backside of Maggie's small farm. She watched and waited, not knowing for what. Scout looked up from the fields and tilted his head and listened and went back to his hunting. With a deep, weary sigh, she turned away. She headed back to the forest. Her hand instinctively reached for Conrí's waiting muzzle at her side. It filled her palm with gratitude, and lifted her heart back to hope.

"Perhaps it's just my belly that needs filling," she rationalized to Conrí. "Perhaps we both are in need of some breakfast," she suggested with growing enthusiasm. The dog responded with a playful trot in complete agreement.

Once back in the woods, and nearing the enchanted center of the forest, Marika began picking wild berries. She still had some bread and milk and potatoes stored in her hut that had been harvested from town a few days earlier.

Filling her skirt front like a basket with the fruit she was finding along their path, she tasted a few samples as they walked. A familiar tang pricked at her tongue and she confided to Conrí, "The berries are turning. A sure sign of the season. I believe they're still acceptable for now – but many a man has lost his legs eating such fruit when they've fermented past this point."

She remembered the wondrous parties and celebrations her *thribli* would be holding about now. The festival of "Samhain" or "All Hallows' Eve" in particular was a time of firelight stories and rituals and legends. Tales that she only half believed, she claimed. But that believing half was ever so careful to not cross the spirits or show disrespect. And the thrill it all brought to the children's bellies was almost as strong as the ale that was brewed and consumed by their elders.

Marika smiled in remembrance and chatted away to Conrí about it the entire way back to the edge of the secret veil. She started to lead them both through the gates.

"I, too, know these festivals," a husky voice almost whispered from a shadow too near.

Marika dropped her skirt edge and berries bounced and rolled in the dirt unheeded at her feet. She held her breath tightly in her chest. Her heartbeat quickened. Conrí sensed her alarm and inserted himself decisively, defensively, between his friend and the shadow.

"The *thribli* celebrates here as well," the voice continued. "The children all hide in their mothers' skirts at the terrible tales of ghosts and goblins. The men challenge each other with drink." A soft chuckle made Marika shiver across her entire body, and her neck felt cold under her thick long hair. She could still not make out a form in the shadow. But she knew.

A width of green silk floated out in a sudden chill breeze.

He stepped slowly forward into the half-light of shade streaked with weak sun. The scarf ruffled in the breeze again. Marika could not take her eyes off of it. Conrí released a low, warning sound from his throat as his upper lip quivered and curled, flashing his sharpest teeth.

"Marika," the man said with a sound of something like satisfaction. He pronounced each syllable as a separate word. He took notice of Conrí and held his place.

Marika ached to turn and run and disappear behind the gates of the protective forest, but refused to lead this evil man into it with her.

"What do you want, Jacko?" she asked as she glared into his face at last, forcing her eyes away from Da's scarf.

"I want you, of course." And he smiled.

"What have you done to my Da?" she asked plainly, knowingly.

"Nothing."

"You wear his scarf," she hissed at him.

He touched it and ran the precious green silk slowly through his coarse, dirty hands without looking down, without letting his eyes leave hers.

"This? This is only to reassure you, Marika. To remind you of your Da's promise to me. No harm has come to your father."

"Da would never – never – give you that scarf!"

"Are you so sure, Marika?" His voice was too soft. "You always were a headstrong child."

"I am not a child," Marika spat back.

"Then stop acting like one!"

He lunged for her, and instinctively, unthinkingly, she slipped through the gates of the secret veil and commanded Conrí to follow. The faithful dog snapped and snarled at the threat, but did as his mistress bade him.

There would be only moments before Jacko would find the entrance and break through.

She ran and leaped and went crashing through clinging branches and brambles and ferns and vines, jumping over fallen logs and jagged rocks and sloping ravines. Conrí's ears pressed back to hear behind them. She stumbled. Her legs and feet were cut and bleeding. Her breath was coming in uneven gasps. She could hear Conrí on her heels. Could she hear Jacko, too?

"Cian ... Fixer ... Whip! Help me!" It was more of a sob than a call. She wasn't even sure where she was anymore. She couldn't see the Bay. She couldn't hear anything but her own heart beating in her ears and Conrí's panting at her side.

"Saoirse!" she called to the Fairy named for freedom. "Please come! Help us! Please ..."

Marika felt herself falling, falling. Almost floating. Blackness was all around her. A hand reached across her mouth. Conrí yelped and was silent. She felt strong hands holding her arms on either side. Then she heard Conrí panting nearby. Was that his tail wagging against her leg? Her eyes adjusted to the semidarkness. The hand slipped from her mouth. Cian's eyes gleamed next to her. Saoirse's whisper in her ear said simply, "Hush!" Marika smelled the soft earth and knew she had been secreted underground again, into a Fairy's quarters. She wept silently in gratitude and steadied her legs under her. She petted Conrí reassuringly. Then, she turned all of her attention to watching Jacko as he came nearer and nearer to the tree root entrance where they were hidden. His boots were so near, loose earth crumbled down on their heads and into their eyes as their upturned faces watched. No one moved. Even Conrí kept absolutely still and silent.

"*Marika!*" Jacko's voice called out with all its tight-muscled strength, and echoed through the entire forest. It wrapped itself around the trunks of trees and bounced off the rocks of the Bay and quivered the leaves overhead. It was followed by a dead silence.

Marika jerked involuntarily in response to that first, rasping, raging, call that was so near them, and Cian's arm wrapped around her shoulders to quiet her.

"*Marika!*" Jacko yelled in the opposite direction. He stomped his large, heavy boots in anger and out-of-control frustration, and pieces of the earth shook and shattered down on them again.

And then she heard the woeful, wonderful sounds from high above. First in the tops of the tallest trees, then drifting down and down, nearer and nearer. The howling and wailing of tortured souls. The rattling of dried bones. The scraping of chains against hard earth and rocks. The whispers, threatening, coming closer, closer.

"Marika! I know it is you in cahoots with these unholy devils," Jacko called loudly, but less sure, more hesitantly.

Snakes appeared, slithering and striking at the man's legs, their fangs sinking into the thick leather of his boots. He kicked at them, flinging them off. And they suddenly changed, shifting into huge, spitting toads and noisy flying insects.

Then, a stunning, piercing, "crack" split the air. Jacko yelled and cursed in pain and spun to see the offending challenger, but found nothing, no one visible. Another "crack." A louder curse. And another "crack" and another and another. More oaths and growls and then stumbling boots – moving away from the underground hiding place.

"Just like your Da, you are," Jacko screamed with rage. "Stubborn and righteous. And wrong!" This last was called with a voice hoarse from anger – but fleeing from the forest. "I will teach you, Marika. I will find you. You cannot keep yourself unseen from me forever. Not from me. I will find you!"

All was silent, then. Saoirse kept patting Marika reassuringly on the back. Cian winked at her and scratched the ears of the dog. But still, they waited. For how long, Marika could not be sure.

At last, soft footfalls padded near. And giggles and snorts and laughing voices.

"Gone, gone. Come up. Come out. The brute is gone – out of the forest. Stinging, and all. We were brilliant!"

The Fairies were all there – all talking at once. Cian and Saoirse brought Marika and Conrí up through the tree roots, right into the center of them.

Conrí remained sniffing and snuffling at the base of the fallen tree from which they had emerged. Marika hugged Cian and Saoirse around their necks until they claimed they couldn't breathe. She tried to thank the other Fairies, but they were congratulating each other so much, she couldn't get a word in. Even Nan and Bob were being agreeable. And Thackeray was laughing too hard to hear any gratitude expressed. It was the only time Marika had seen him laugh – or smile, for that matter. And she watched him, watched them all, through warm, quiet tears.

Her relief was deep and genuine. But her heart remained uneasy. Her soul restless with a feeling she could not name. She did not consciously acknowledge nor dare recognize doubt.

It was approaching midnight. Soon after Marika's rescue, a spontaneous celebration had broken out and had been progressing for hours.

Over the course of the evening, the entire gathering of Fairies introduced Marika to a side of their society she had only heard of in fables. And all was true, she was learning. All was smashingly true.

Campfires were glowing in circles of magical light. Their flames cast shadows that were deep and long and walked among the edges of the night. They seemed to move in and out of the forest along with the Fairies themselves until Marika could hardly tell one from the other, reality from illusion.

Laughter and chatter filled the air and floated across the tops of the trees like a thousand bells ringing in harmony and unison. Yet, to the outsider, all that could be heard was the wind through the pines – singing, whistling, gentle to the ear. An oddly familiar sound, something remembered from childhood.

As Marika had remarked to Conrí just hours earlier, fermented berries were at the heart of much of the gaiety. Bowls and bowls of the tangy fruit were passed continuously from hand to hand. In addition, from deep beneath the ground, large wooden barrels were rolled to the surface, each filled with a stout, brown beer that had been brewed with a special Fairies' touch and temperament.

"Look out, look out, my dears," Fixer called as the barrels of ale were followed by thick pottery jugs that sloshed from side to side with beautiful, deeply colored wines wrought from fat wild grapes and aged to a delicious and powerful peak. "Oh, do be careful, *careful!*" Fixer fussed at the bearers. "You're spilling it everywhere – and you know what it does to the mealy bugs," he said with raised eyebrows, a finger laid beside his nose, and a tisk of his tongue. And then he laughed out loud. A rather naughty sounding laugh, Marika thought.

Just then, Marika was nudged gently aside as Wee Ann was directing the delivery of massive platters of a variety of lovely looking foodstuff. All had been well prepared and stored for just such an occasion and was now being brought forward and laid out with great ceremony.

"Just here," Wee Ann called. "And here. And here." Marika was a bit surprised to see the tiny spirit use such authority. But the other Fairies obliged her with good humor and efficiency and somewhat excessive amounts of chatting. All across the tops of smooth flat tree stumps, or on level open clearings of the forest floor itself, they placed the filled plates and bowls until there was hardly an empty space between them.

There were cakes and meat pies and fruits. Sweets that defied description. Roasted nuts and wild berries. Steaming potatoes and stuffed rolled grape leaves. And every type of bean and root imaginable. Corn nuggets and radishes and bits of many things Marika didn't quite recognize. The young girl politely asked about some of the dishes she had never seen before, but the Fairies were quite secretive, disinclined to share their recipes. Thackeray, it turned out, was one of the best chefs in the entire forest. It was difficult to not thank him, Marika found when she tasted some of his wares. But his pride was evident without the praise.

Throughout the night, fantastic, mesmerizing music was almost constant. Marika marveled at the ingenious instruments, as well as the expert musicianship. She heard magical flutes and pine needle zithers and hollow wooden clackers and drums. Some played wind chimes and acorn castanets and whistles made of wild green grasses. There were violins carved from ancient oak, with strings and bows of silvery spun spider webs – and the sounds they produced were evocative of baby's laughter one minute and a widow's tears the next. Hand-held accordions breathed luscious melodies from supple magnolia leaves bound together with slivers of dried grasses. Bagpipes created from woven strips of green tree bark and long straight water reeds were thoroughly haunting and echoed through the entire forest.

And Marika sang.

Marika's Gran often told her that if the presence of Fairies could ever be detected by an outsider, it would be through their music. "So unique and mystical it is," she would say. "It slips into the very soul of a being and holds it utterly captive. Oh yes, my dear, music is the private, personal realm of the true Fairy." And tonight, Marika understood. Even her own magical singing was rivaled by that night's haunting, hypnotic sounds.

But beyond the music, there were games and entertainment of every talent. Marika first noticed that she hadn't seen Cian and his Water Fairies for quite some time. Then, with a thrilling fanfare of fluttering flutes, Cian emerged from the depths of the center of the Bay, surrounded by a rising troupe of dancers. They were spotlighted by the very moon itself. The stars fell about their shoulders. In silver haze and moonbeams, they twisted and turned and dove through the water with stunning athletic grace and enchanting design. Their movements recounted ancient stories and myths. Their bodies somehow became imbued with the music. Marika was completely mesmerized by them. She was still catching her breath and clapping enthusiastically when the final dance came to a climax and, within the next moment, Cian was at her side, laughing over her obvious enjoyment.

"Cian, you were brilliant!" she said. "It was the loveliest dance I have ever witnessed – even compared to the most talented gypsies. I've never seen anything so amazing!"

"And who do you think taught the gypsies their trade?" Cian replied, shaking a few drops of starlight off of his hair and wiping his brow with a nearby leaf. "The student has yet to overtake the master," he concluded in truth more than pride.

Marika wanted to express more of her pleasure, but could not be heard for the raucous laughter created by the Fairies who were Shifters and their hilarious mimicry that was just then taking place. They began by imitating Thackeray being thanked, complete with cursing and muttering that sounded remarkably as if it were in his own voice. They stamped their feet and tore their clothing and hair and threw themselves bodily into the crowd. The audience, including Thackeray, roared with appreciation and tossed them back to their feet with cries for more. So they quickly began depicting a scene where Nan and Bob were forced to tell the truth – a cunning bit of verbal trickery and plenty of play on words. This eventually segued into a one-act play about wild birds nibbling unwittingly on fermented berries, where feathers flew and Marika decided she would never look at an egg in the same way again. They even performed a skit about Marika rescuing Conrí from his bed of thorns, emphasizing her obvious clumsiness that resulted in her own injuries and her heart that never could let a creature suffer within her sight or hearing. Their humor was biting, but not unkind. Centered on truth, it was edged in imagination and polished in originality. By the time they got to a rather remarkable interpretation of Jacko and his last, ignoble exit from the forest, everyone was holding their sides with mirth.

Things quieted then, the fires were stirred, the shadows deepened, and Wee Ann climbed to the top of a low tree stump. She stood in the glow of the flames and folded her dainty hands behind her. She cleared her throat twice, and recited a bit of original poetry. It was perfectly lovely and quaint and everyone smiled, gently clapping their hands and snapping their fingers, but then she became terribly embarrassed and had to hide in the forest thickets for almost an hour.

As the drink and food continued to flow, and the fires crackled around husky-voiced laughter, Thackeray made the rounds, displaying smooth and clever sleight-of-hand, some right under Marika's nose – and she never could quite see how it was done. Others performed juggling tricks and acrobatics and physical stunts as they wound their way through the crowd and the night. Nan and Bob gathered everyone around them, sat near the central fire, and told grand and convincing tales. They acted out the most intriguing parts, employing props and bits of costumes – even Conrí at one point.

Quite naturally, some of the local forest animals joined in the revelry as well. "Oh Lord, don't give any fermented berries or beer to the raccoons," Cian wailed as he saw them coming. "They're ever so cross and downright mean when they're drunk." Marika laughed and vowed she would do her part to make sure none of the rascals neared the stuff.

"Mind you," Cian continued, "under the same conditions, the squirrels do a slap dance that is not to be missed." Immediately, Marika served the first ones she could find a bit of the juice just to witness the phenomenon for herself.

The woodland deer, shy creatures by nature, crept near and quickly joined in the spirit of the evening, allowing any who wished a ride on their backs through the moonlit forest. Marika approached the buck who seemed to be the alpha animal of his pack and marveled at his immense and regal looking crown of antlers. "Would you be so kind as to grant me a ride about the clearing," she asked with a slight curtsy. He gallantly nodded his assent. She climbed gently onto his back and felt his warmth rise and surround her entire body. He turned his head to look into her eyes, and she had to duck under his great and gleaming headdress. Then, he sprang effortlessly into a smooth, quick gait. She wondered at his elegant gliding motion, so unlike the rhythmic bounce of a horse, which she had somewhat expected. They ran as if they were one with the wind; the night flowed and billowed through her long thick hair; the moonlight shimmered before them. She closed her eyes and felt as if she were flying on unseen wings – floating across the face of the earth, certain that if she looked down she would see the tops of the trees beneath their feet and the Bay a shining circle below. At last, she felt the buck slowing his pace, and she began to let her eyes open. Peeking through her lashes, she found herself returned to the same spot where they had begun, and the music was once again filling her ears. She slid to the ground, and thanked the grand and gracious animal with a soft stroke to his ears. *"Go raibh maith agaibh,"* she whispered in Gaelic to thank him. And, of course, he understood. She stopped long enough to also pet the warm silky head of his eldest fawn, and then returned to the center of the celebration.

Whether it was the strength of the drink, the lateness of the hour, or just the personality of the beasts, the bears who had joined the party eventually got terribly solemn and solitary and went off alone to sulk in the outer reaches of the woods. The owls of the forest were rather judgmental and openly disapproved of the entire celebration. But no one paid particular attention to them and just let them hoot alone. The majority of the other creatures of the woods, Marika noted, preferred to simply watch.

The music played on and everyone danced and danced and danced. They drank and ate until they could hold no more. The stories got bolder. The songs became bawdier. And the fires fell to mere embers. By the time the night stars were wandering their way back home behind the clouds, and the dawn was peeking over the rim of the forest to see what it had missed, most of the Fairies were well in their cups.

"Good night, Cian," Marika finally yawned as she stumbled

toward her small hut for an hour or two of sleep.

Cian giggled back.

"Are you all right?" she asked, knowing her friend had repeatedly leaned into the drink with an empty cup.

"Very," he replied with too much dignity. "Oh, excuse me ... I believe that was me."

Marika, who had refrained from partaking of any strong drink herself – except for a sip or two of beer for good health, as Gran would have cautioned – was only suffering from lack of sleep and too much dancing. But she was among the minority, she realized, as she and Conrí began to slowly survey the damage all around them while they picked their way back to the hut.

There was a great deal of rather loud, unrestrained snoring from all parts of the forest. There were Fairies and creatures cast about over rocks and logs and thick tree roots. They were flat on their backs or curled into cramped little balls. Some were in trees. Some were draped across floating leaves and pinecones. A few were in places where they quite frankly never should have been. The Bay and its surrounding woods looked simply shameful.

"Good night, Cian," Marika called out again. "Come on Conrí. I fear we'll all be feeling this night in the light of day – which is fast approaching. And some of us surely more than others."

In the distance, Marika heard a quiet mumble, "That, of course, is Irish for saying a simple goodnight." It was followed by, "G'night, Luv. Sleep .... Oh, dear ... I seem to have stepped in something." Then, a sloppy splash into the Bay. And all was silent.

Within a few minutes, Marika and Conrí were fast asleep in her snug little hut. Only Conrí awoke, lifted his head, and watched with intelligent eyes when Aisling, the dream Fairy, appeared just a few yards away from them. Her image faded slowly in and out, light to dark, clear to murky. At first, her gentle smile foretold, it seemed,

of peace and joyful days ahead. But then it shaded into deep, chill,
shadows that made her countenance turn a frightful, impenetrable,
black. Conrí made a whimpering sound in his throat and inched
closer to Marika's side, but she did not stir.

Christmas.

A clear sort of sparkle had threaded its way through the air over the few weeks leading up to Christmas, and it quickened all the life of the forest – indeed the entire town as well. Creatures of all kinds scampered about, rustling, hustling. Even the sun hurried across the earth, barely touching the Bay on its way. The sky was translucent, with clouds that scurried to and from the horizons, leaving mere milky trails behind them.

Much of the forest was evergreen and would retain a subdued lushness throughout the entire winter. The holly berries had become bright blood red and their shining green leaves poked playfully at passersby. Pine needles scented the air and stretched their fingers as far as they would reach, sticky with pinecones and golden sap. There were even a few delicate southern blossoms that burst forth at just this time of year – an unexpected treat for Marika, who adored the earth and all its blessings. But many of the trees and bushes did put their finery away for the season and slept in their plain brown skins until the spring warmth would call them awake again, and coax out their colors and cooling shade.

The sun was late in rising and early to bed now; not long overhead, taking a shortcut across the sky. One afternoon, Marika and Conrí had been enjoying an exploratory stroll through the far side of the forest when the sun seemed to disappear right before their eyes.

This particular day had begun with an entirely different air about it – oppressive and moist and too warm. It was almost hard to breathe. The daylight had been working with difficulty to thrust itself through thick mists and curling fogs that rolled up from the Bay and the very ground itself. Apparently, Marika told Conrí, the sun was simply too weak from the effort to remain for a long goodbye. And so, without any warning, it was gone, dropped over the edge of the earth.

There was no moon that night, and the persistent fog and mists seemed to have joined forces with the clouds to make sure the stars would not be of any assistance to the travelers as well. To her great surprise and personal embarrassment, Marka found herself quite suddenly, quite thoroughly, lost. Understanding her unspoken need, Conrí took over the lead.

They were nearing that part of the forest where Marika had first encountered Conrí in the evil bundle of thorns. Both of them sensed the spot, and were being especially careful to avoid any contact with it.

Then, a terrible, unholy wail engulfed them. They stopped and listened – listened with their entire bodies as well as their ears.

They were cries for help. And again they came. Pleas for death. Prayers for God to take this pitiful creature's life. The voice seemed somehow familiar to Marika, but she could not be sure. It was that of a man; a black man; a slave.

The girl had never heard such pain in a human voice. She could not react, her body froze in its place. Even Conrí held his footing beside her; but he let out a low, moaning howl in return.

The voice cried out again, pleading for death to come quickly, weeping, in agony. At first, it seemed to be only a few yards ahead of them – and then it came from somewhere to their left – and again from behind where they stood. Marika tried to take a cautious step forward – perhaps she could find the source. Perhaps she could help this poor suffering man. She had to try. But, quickly and decisively, Conrí positioned himself in front of her legs, barring her way.

"Look out, Conrí," she scolded softly. "Let me move." But Conrí held his body firmly across the front of her legs. When she tried to step around him, he realigned himself in front of her again. When she attempted to dislodge him by pushing him aside, he stood rooted to the spot.

"Conrí! What are you doing?" she cried slightly louder and more firmly. "Conrí, move! Let me pass," she commanded. "We must try to help him." The dog would not obey.

The tortured man groaned in pain and torment. "We must help, Conrí. Please let me go to him," Marika pleaded with the dog. Still, he would not move.

Just as Marika was pushing hard on the dog's side without any understanding of or patience for his actions, another sound reached her ears out of the distant darkness. A horse was approaching. Walking, slowly, cautiously. The murky thickness of the mist reflected a lantern as well.

She was about to call out when the fog parted slightly and the light of the lamp fell briefly across the face of its bearer: Jacko.

Her voice stopped in her throat. She stood absolutely silent and still. Her fear of this man paralyzed her compassion for the other, injured one. All she could do was wait, with Conrí leaning protectively, yet shivering, against her knees.

"Ho! Who are you? What is the matter with you?" Jacko's voice growled into the darkness toward the moaning man. But all had grown ominously silent.

Then the voice wavered pitiably: "Please, sir...kill me...please."

"A man likes to know who he's killing ... and why," Jacko answered back. He had dismounted, and held the lantern high in his left hand as he swung it to and fro searching for the source of the voice. "Where are you? Who are you?" he repeated as he looked all around.

Marika held her breath, fearing the lantern's glow might pierce the fog and reach her in the darkness before it had found the injured man. But the light was held at bay by the mist as it crept and swirled around her and Conri.

The voice called out again, pleading, asking if Jacko was an angel of death sent to take him out of his pain.

"Don't talk stupid. Just keep making noise so I can find you," Jacko responded in a voice that exhibited no compassion, only growing annoyance. He walked slowly toward the apparent origin of the cries. But the fog bounced and refracted the sounds so that they seemed to come from no specific point and even move about.

"I said talk!" Jacko commanded harshly.

The voice responded with cries for mercy and pity. It was the sound of a soul's anguish, Marika thought. And the sound of a mind no longer a part of its body. The words turned to sobbing, and then she recognized it. These were the same mournful cries she remembered from a small, rank cabin on a nearby plantation. It was Ishmael! Poor, tortured Ishmael – now caught in this hideous tangle of thorns. Marika's heart broke at the thought that she had not been able to find him – to help him – before Jacko had arrived. With baseless hope she thought perhaps Jacko would free him, would help him, would release him from this terrible trap.

At that moment, Jacko at last found Ishmael. When Marika saw him in the swinging light of the lantern, a flash from a long, sharp knife blade reflected from Jacko's hand. He lifted it high over Ishmael's head.

"I know you," he said with a dead, low voice. "A slave to Isaac Winston, you are. A runaway slave caught in his own escape. Guess the 'god' you been calling to for help doesn't want you running any more – doesn't want you to be free," Jacko tormented Ishmael with his words.

Marika bit her lip to keep herself silent. Conrí pressed harder against her legs as a reminder to hold her place.

"Please, sir ... kill me," Ishmael called again hoarsely through his tears.

Jacko moved in with his knife. He raised it higher. Marika sucked in her breath to scream. Jacko stepped forward. The lantern swung across his black eyes. Marika leaped over Conrí's back and began to run toward them. Conrí's teeth caught her skirt. "Please kill me!" the voice wept. Jacko laughed, as he cut the vines that imprisoned the man.

"And why would I be killing a perfectly good slave, now?" his harsh voice asked. "Perhaps I have better plans for you."

Marika stopped suddenly and held her place as she held her breath. She watched Jacko free Ishmael completely from the torturing vines. She watched as he lifted the bleeding man first to his own strong back, and then to the back of his horse, where the slave sat slumped, spiritless. She watched as Jacko led them out of the forest. She listened as the fog closed around them and muffled their retreat – with Jacko saying cunningly: "Everything will be different now, Slave. Now, you belong to me."

After a long while, Marika let Conrí lead her back to their hut. Her heart was heavy with shame that she had not helped Ishmael herself – that she had let her own personal fear keep her from doing what was right. Her head was thick with confusion over Jacko's actions. She could not trust his motives, could not understand his intentions. Her soul cried out to God to watch over Ishmael. Sad, imprisoned, Ishmael, who had prayed to God to die – and was saved instead, perhaps by the devil himself.

Marika embraced Conrí for a long time with gratitude for his insight and loyalty. They ate silently around the small campfire she built, and then she climbed onto the pallet of pinestraw in the far corner of her hut. Conrí positioned himself, as always, across its opening.

Marika slept as fitfully as the fog that swirled and undulated around them throughout the night. The Bay was strangely silent. She had not sung even one song that evening. Nor had she encountered a single Fairy. For some reason, she felt compelled to promise herself that she would move underground soon – as the Fairies had been begging her to do for many months. And, sooner still, she thought, she wanted to see Joseph.

Perhaps it was the pure strength of Marika's desire to see Joseph that carried the impulse to do so to him. Perhaps it was simply because that day – a day that dawned clear and bright – was Christmas Eve. But soon after the sun reached its zenith in a cloudless sky, Marika heard Joseph's voice calling to her at the secret gates. Her heart leapt and she gathered a few small things from the hut and signaled to Conrí, who was hunting on the far side of the Bay. He quickly caught up with her as she broke through the veil and raced into the open arms of a smiling Joseph.

"It's about time, Child," he pretended to scold. "I've been calling you 'til I thought you weren't coming. Just about to give up and move on."

"I came running as fast as my legs would be carrying me, as well you know," Marika responded with equal levity. "And I brought Conrí to be seeing you and all."

"Brought him? Child, you can't take two steps without him on your heels, and you know *that!*"

"And sometimes I can't even take two steps *because* of him," she replied, thinking of the night when he had held her back from danger.

"Joseph, there's something I want to be telling you," she began hesitantly.

"And whatever it is, I want to hear about it. But can it wait for one minute? I have something important to share with you, too," he replied.

"Yes, Joseph. What is it?" She was almost concerned at his demeanor – a sort of excitement lightly cloaked with nervousness. It was exceedingly unlike him.

"What is it?" she repeated.

"It's Christmas Eve," he whispered conspiratorially.

"I know," she whispered back.

"I have a gift for you," he said leaning into her ear as his voice got even quieter. "May I give it to you now?"

Marika nodded shyly but enthusiastically. "Yes, please."

Joseph gave a quick sharp whistle, and his horse came out from behind a clump of nearby trees. And there, sitting on the animal's back, was Maggie. Her hand covered her mouth, which quivered with smiles and weeping – not certain which way it wanted to go.

Marika's eyes filled with tears. Suddenly, no trace remained of the bitterness she had so carefully guarded and kept polished in her heart for those long months of separation.

"Oh, Miss," Marika sighed as she stumbled into Maggie's embrace.

The older woman's feet had barely touched the ground from the horse and she was dancing the young girl all about her. First, she clutched her close and they wept and both tried to talk at once. In the next moment, Maggie pushed the girl back, holding her at arm's length and scolded into the air for how thin she thought her to be. Then, Marika was pulled in again, so tightly her breath was muffled in Maggie's soft bodice and cape. Then, pushed back for more critical study and claims over her beauty and color of cheek and hair. The third tug forward forced Joseph to intervene: "Miss Maggie! You'll shake the child in two. Let her catch her wind and get her legs under her! Come here, sit, both of you," he laughed.

They each took a seat on either side of Joseph, Marika on a thick worn root of a sheltering tree, Maggie sharing the newly fallen log where Joseph was already waiting.

Maggie dabbed at her eyes with a bit of a hankie she had tucked up her sleeve. Joseph pulled his large, clean kerchief from his back pocket and waved it in front of Marika, but her sleeve itself finished the job before she noticed it. Then she took it from him out of courtesy, blew decisively, and handed it back.

"Well," Joseph began, "Happy Christmas one and all." He laughed heartily into the clear air.

Without words, but a broad smile on her face, Maggie stood and walked over to the horse and pulled a large package from one of the saddlebags. It was wrapped carefully in brown paper and string. She presented it to Marika saying, "I made this for you. I hope it fits. If you're going to be spending the winter in the forest, you'll need to keep warm."

As Marika anxiously tugged at the strings, more tears curved down her rose-red cheeks and collected at the corners of her smile. "Thank you, Miss. Oh, thank you," she whispered before she had even unwrapped the soft contents.

At last, a fluffy, bright red, knit sweater appeared, and Marika's eyes were aglow. "For me, Miss? You made this just for me?" She lovingly lifted the garment from its protective wrapper and held it up in front of her.

"Try it on, Dear," Maggie encouraged.

Marika's head was lost for long moments in thick folds of red wool, but eventually popped out at the top. Her arms squiggled through the sleeves, and the body of the sweater swung freely over her back and chest. Her face was all smiles as she flapped the long sleeves up and down, while the hem of the thing hung well below her knees.

Maggie squinted and leaned back to look.

Joseph suppressed a smile. "Could be a mite big, I'm thinking," he finally offered.

"I thought she'd have grown over the months," Maggie replied. "Perhaps I over estimated."

But Marika just rolled up the sleeves into large cuffs and beamed. "It's the most beautiful sweater ever there was!" she said with conviction. And thus, it became so.

Joseph then produced from one of his jacket pockets another parcel done up with brown paper and twine. But this one was smaller and oblong in shape.

"I thought you could use these," he said with an understanding wink as he handed it to Marika.

Marika's fingers trembled with anticipation as she untied the string and unfurled the paper. There, lying in a profusion of every color imaginable, were lengths and lengths of hair ribbons. They gleamed of satin and silk, fine grosgrain and lace. Marika wound them over her hands and held them against her cheeks and her tears darkened their colors.

"Thank you, Joseph," she finally whispered. "Da and Gran and Danny... and then Thackeray..." but she couldn't finish.

"I know, Child," he answered simply.

"Here," he cleared his voice and said a little too loudly as he pulled another package from inside his coat. "This one's for that creature that follows you everywhere."

Marika carefully folded the ribbons back into their wrapping and reached for the gift for Conrí. She pulled back the paper and lifted out a soft leather collar made of beautifully tanned hide. And perfectly etched down one side was Conrí's name. A shinning silver buckle glistened at one end.

"Conrí, look!" Marika held it out for her friend to sniff and explore. "All your own, and such a handsome bit of neckwear it is! You shall look every bit the king by the wearing of it." And with that, Marika strapped it around Conrí's waiting neck. He shook it into place and pranced around the party knowing he had been given a very special prize.

"How lovely you have both been to me," Marika smiled at her two friends. "Thank you for both of us," she grinned. "Thank you with all my heart."

But before either Joseph or Maggie could respond, she said, "And I just might be having a bit of something to give to each of you as well," she giggled.

She reached behind her and brought forward a small brown leather book, wiped it smooth and clean on her skirt, and handed it lovingly to Joseph.

"What is this, Child?" Joseph responded with genuine wonder. He began to turn the pages and carefully examine the drawings and writing on the first few sheets. As he read, his face became alight with smiles and understanding.

Marika jumped up at that point and went to sit next to him and peer over his shoulder. "They're special *Fairy* (she whispered the word away from Maggie) potions and spells," she said. "For curing and healing, you see."

"Yes," he said with awe, "I do see."

"I drew the pictures of the plants and ingredients myself. The *Fairies* (again, whispered) helped me get the mixtures just right. And I wrote them down exactly."

She continued with seriousness but excitement in her voice: "These are just for you, Joseph. Now you have your own book of medicine and learning that even Doc doesn't know. Now, you have *more* learning than himself!" She finished with great pride on Joseph's behalf.

Joseph kept turning the pages and noting one entry after another. He remarked on several, showing them to Maggie, who had great appreciation for the folk remedies as well.

"Who did she say helped with these?" Maggie tried to ask. But Joseph's look stopped her inquiry.

"Marika – this is the most wonderful book – an amazing gift," Joseph enthused. "I can't wait to really study it. I shall treasure it forever." And he reached up and patted her hand where it lay on his shoulder. "Thank you, Child."

Marika then hiked her new sweater up to her waist and reached deeply into the pocket of her skirt. She withdrew something large and glittering that she cupped in both hands. "I meant to give this to you, Joseph, to give to Maggie. But here she is sitting so near ... and it's good to be putting it into her own hands for myself." Shyly, Marika reached for Maggie's folded hands, and placed in them a heavy, beautifully carved, man's pocket watch.

Maggie looked down, examined the treasure, and said, "Why, it's my husband's pocket watch. I thought it was lost. I thought it was ... how did you ... when did you ...?"

Joseph leaned over to her and said softly: "I find it best not to ask."

Marika said with enthusiasm, "Listen to it," and she lifted it from Maggie's hands to her ear. It ticked with regularity and certainty and,

Maggie noted, it was keeping perfect time.

"But this watch hasn't worked for years – not since my husband passed away. It couldn't be repaired I was told," Maggie said as she looked back and forth between Joseph and Marika.

"How did you ... how did she...?"

"I have a friend who fixes things quite handily," was all Marika revealed.

"Oh, Marika! You can't know how this pleases me," Maggie cried as she embraced the girl. Never again would she ask how the watch had come into Marika's possession, nor who her capable friend was.

The rest of the afternoon was spent with much laughter and treats. Maggie had brought apples and cinnamon sticks and hard striped candies. Joseph produced chestnuts that they roasted on the fire he built. They made tea and drank it steaming hot from small round cups that Maggie had furnished. Marika had even convinced the Fairy "Yum" to spare a few small cakes that were as light as spun sugar and sparkled in the sun.

The only slight break in the perfect gaiety of the day was when Joseph reminded Marika that she had said she had something of importance to say to him when they first met that afternoon. As he broached the subject, her smile faded and her eyes grew dark. She thought for just a moment and replied: "I just wanted to tell you how much I've been missing you, that's all."

He looked quizzically into her eyes, but saw there would be nothing more forthcoming. Perhaps she would tell him later, he believed. But in Marika's own heart, she knew the secret about Jacko and Ishmael and the bed of thorns would remain untold. She could not have said or even understood why, but she protected the secret itself as much as she protected Joseph and Maggie from it.

And so they returned to telling each other great stories of Christmases past, and simply enjoying each other's company.

126

Too soon, the winter sun was sliding and slipping below the trees and then beyond the horizon.

The three friends hugged one another with much affection. There were warm tears and loving words and promises of more visits to come. Then Joseph helped Maggie to the back of his horse, took the reins in hand, and reluctantly turned and left the forest.

Marika and Conrí watched and lingered there until their companions were far from sight or hearing. Then they stepped quickly behind the secret veil.

That night, with a full and loving heart, the young girl sang all the Christmas songs she knew, to all the Fairies she had come to know – some now cherished perhaps even more than the *thribli* she had left behind, seemingly so long, long ago. She snuggled down to bed with the prized red sweater wrapped tightly around her, and fell asleep trying to decide which of her glorious new hair ribbons she would wear on Christmas Day.

But Marika had kept her greatest gifts to both Joseph and Maggie a very special surprise. Exactly as she had negotiated with Aisling, the gifts were delivered personally to each of the two friends that night. Shortly before dawn, as each lay in deep and peaceful sleep, Aisling brought to them a perfect dream – a dream in which Marika sang a singularly beautiful, meaningful, song of Christmas joy. In turn, each recipient stirred slightly and sighed contentedly. And the first light of Christmas morning kissed the world awake.

Christmas Day was bright with sunshine and expectations.

Early that morning, Marika created a warm, crackling fire in the center of her old peninsula. Then she sorted through her collection of special items that she kept safely contained in a cigar box she had found one day obviously abandoned on the edge of a back porch step near town. From the corner of the box she retrieved a lovely fat square of barely used soap. This particular prize had been waiting for her on the top of a washstand set out in the center of a large backyard in the heart of town. A comfortable looking black woman had been using it on the clothes she was laundering, when she had been called into the house suddenly – although perhaps not unexpectedly – by the squall and screams of two unseen quarreling children. Marika remembered how the woman had muttered to herself as she hastily dried her hands on her apron and hurried up the back porch stairs into the house to settle the disagreement. There had, in fact, been two squares of the smooth, white washing soap waiting on the stand. And Marika had only taken the one – the partially used one at that. She had also repositioned the pole that was supporting the hanging line so that the sheets already laid on it were lifted clear of the ground. And she had chased off the geese as they were heading to the washtub to inquire about it in the absence of the washer woman. In return for the favors, Marka felt she had been extremely fair in the trade for the single, partially used, soap bar.

Christmas morning indeed warranted a wash for herself as well as her clothes, she had decided. Fortunately, in this temperate climate, she was pleasantly surprised at the feel of the water in the Bay as it closed over her disrobed body. She used the soap with vigor and felt ever so much the better for it. She splashed and dove and swam as she had not done since the beginning of winter. Even her long, thick, dark auburn hair got a deep scrubbing with soap as well.

While she was still submerged, she began pulling the clothing that she had piled on the nearby banks into the Bay with her, one piece at a time, and scrubbed them smartly against a large, flat rock. Socks and skirts, shirts and knickers, all got a thorough going over.

A few of the Water Babies came to the surface to see what was making such a stir of their home, but soon they were all splashing and giggling and playing happily with the soap bubbles the girl created for them, and trying their best to help.

Marika had carefully kept the red sweater that Maggie had given her for Christmas warming near the fire. She hastily climbed out of the Bay and pulled its soft, thick covering over her slightly shivering body. Then she twisted the excess water from the freshly washed clothing – some having been wrestled good-naturedly from the grip of a teasing Water Fairy – and laid them out to dry on several thick logs she had arranged for this purpose around the fire. She hung a few of the items in the sun on low-reaching tree branches.

As she sat on a large tree root near the fire to dry her beautiful hair, she began to sing. And many of the Fairies came to join her and listen to her praises to God on this glorious, holy morning.

Before long, the clean fresh clothes were thoroughly dry and folded and tucked neatly back into her carpetbag, and she was wearing her best blue skirt beneath the new red sweater. Even her shoes had been cleaned and polished almost to a shine by Wee Ann. A bright red ribbon graced her hair.

Marika was cordially invited to join the Fairies in their traditional celebration of Christmas Day. She found it delightful, albeit a bit different from what her own people would be doing.

There was no special decorating for the season, she noticed, but thoroughly understood why there would not be. After all, the Fairies' home was the sacred forest itself – luscious fir trees at every turn, each bright with perching birds for color and song; holly berries and mistletoe naturally hanging on bushes and branches all around them. Even the doorways to their living quarters were edged in pinecones and wreathed in evergreens every day, not just for this special occasion.

Although the Fairies eat their fill of wondrous delights every day, and celebrate together at frequent banquets regardless of the date, they brought Marika to join them for their Christmas meal, which by tradition was hosted beneath the shade of the oldest tree in the forest. For the past one hundred and thirty-seven years, this annual holiday banquet tree was an ancient cypress, so immense from age that its arms embraced a wider expanse than any tree Marika had ever seen. By the time they arrived, its low hanging branches looked like the broad stooping shoulders of an indulgent grandfather. Fairies were everywhere. The giant tree's swollen bumpy knees rose up from the surrounding ground as well, providing additional seating for even more guests. Some of the massive knotted roots of the tree offered long bench-like surfaces for the laying out of food and the propping up of drink barrels. And the many twists and turns of its age-scarred trunk cradled perfect hiding places for any number of surprises.

The exchanging of Christmas gifts was conspicuously absent. This was, Marika discovered, something uniquely human; in truth, a rather foreign concept to the Fairy culture. Quite coincidentally, Wee Ann had left a lovely large red button at the entrance to Marika's hut that morning. It was found, the Fairy said, just the day before, and she had thought immediately that Marika might enjoy putting it on Danny's grave when next she went to call. This was the true spirit and manner in which Fairies typically give gifts, Marika learned. Whenever one found or created something that they thought another would like or could use, they simply gave it to that recipient right away. To put it aside for giving later – especially on just one designated day – seemed rude to them, delaying and denying pleasure to the intended receiver for no good reason at all.

Fairies, on the whole, absolutely delight in giving gifts – especially surprise gifts – to each other as well as to outsiders. But, they believe very logically: how surprised can anyone be if gifts are

130

given only on a specified day?

"No, no," they shook their heads. "The human tradition of Christmas and birthday gifts is absurd." And they all agreed with each other: "Our way is much, much better."

Somewhat to her own surprise, Marika thought they were probably right.

In addition to the collaborative banquet, a great deal of seasonal greetings and good wishes rang out all across the enchanted forest that day. They floated over the Bay and echoed through the clearings and wove themselves around stands of trees. Even the animals of the woods shared the good will and joy in the air. The birds sang just a bit more brightly. The squirrels chattered and teased and circled the trunks of the trees with high good humor and a grand spirit of fun. At the same time, the mice refrained from stealing bits of anyone's grain. The rabbits felt free to roam, unafraid of anything untoward happening. Even the spiders rolled up their webs out of harm's way and kept from collecting so much as a dew drop in their nets for the entire day.

Following the feast, Marika sang some more and the Fairies played their magical flutes and harmonicas, their bagpipes and drums. It was a day of absolute peace. A day when love for all creatures filled hearts and embraced one and all.

Marika rejoiced with the Fairy gathering and forest beings throughout the day, and greatly enjoyed their company. But still, her soul was restless and hollow somehow. In the end, she realized that she sorely felt the absence of Danny and Gran and her Da.

For the first time since she had left Boston, she missed her family – her *thribli* – with an intense, almost overwhelming, longing.

Approaching sundown, Marika and Conrí left the Fairy gathering and traveled unobtrusively into town. All along the soft dirt roads, there moved carriages filled with laughing people, some snuggling children on their laps, all holding smiles snuggly on their faces. The horses were decorated with sleigh bells edging their harnesses, and they pranced with vigor just to hear them jingle.

The homes in town were aglow with lamplight and hearth fires and happiness. Doors stood open wide to welcome visitors. Candles peered out from every window, signaling to strangers who might be angels in disguise. Music drifted everywhere.

Marika's journey eventually found her and Conrí outside an old stone church, crouched beneath an exquisitely crafted stained-glass window. The front doors to the building were held open by slabs of gray, roughhewn rock. The voices of the singing congregation washed over Marika and the dog on the breath of holy incense. A small organ wheezed along with the tune in a cheerful yet reverent sort of way. She had found the local Catholic church – and remembered the priest's voice from Danny's funeral. The familiarity of the Christmas mass enveloped her as she hunched on the ground against the smooth stone wall and held Conrí close, under one arm.

When the last prayer had been sent to God, and the last parishioner had been sent home, Marika pulled her shawl across her head, slipped through the doorway, and worked her way along the outside edge of a far side aisle to the front of the sanctuary. There, she knelt in the shadow of the cross and lit a candle for Danny, one for Gran, and one for Da. Then she lit one for Ishmael. She had no coins, no pennies to pay for the candles. But she carefully left the red button in the collection box.

Conrí padded down the aisle behind her as they left. The priest stood watching silently in the shadows.

It was well into evening when Marika and Conrí reached Danny's grave. But a full Carolina moon lighted their way as brightly as if it had been midday. A heaven full of stars all flickered and glittered so near that Marika wanted to reach out and fetch one down to place on the stone that marked Danny's place on earth.

Conrí stood watch over Marika, who had stretched out on her back side-by-side next to her brother. While she tracked the moon across the sky, she told Danny about all the adventures she had been having recently. She gave him every detail of the party in the forest. She recounted the Christmas celebration of the day before with Joseph – and the reconciliation with Maggie. She apologized for not having the red button from Wee Ann to leave for him. Then she reached into her pocket and took out a carefully folded piece of paper. Rolling over on her stomach, she smoothed the paper out on the top of the grave and explained the drawing on it to the boy.

"This is to prove that I really am living among the Fairies – just in case you weren't believing me," she said. "I've made a drawing of them. Here's Cian, and Thackeray, and Wee Ann, and Fixer," she named the spirits as she tapped their images with her finger. "They're awfully difficult to draw, actually, because they move about and change so quickly," she explained. "But I thought you'd like to have this picture anyway."

She folded the thin paper into squares that got smaller and smaller until she could fold it no more. Then she placed it near the top of the grave, and weighted it with a stone.

Assuring herself that they were quite alone, she spoke Shelta softly to Danny about how much she loved and missed him. She recited a prayer in their familiar Irish. And she sang Danny's favorite Christmas carol about the baby Jesus.

As the last notes were still caressing the tops of the trees and clinging to the edges of the graves, she lifted herself to her knees and kissed Danny's headstone. She stood, then, and wished him a final Happy Christmas, and returned slowly to the forest with Conrí not two steps behind.

Going To Ground.

The very earth itself was infused with music. The sound lovingly stroked the roots of the trees and dipped into the waters below. It was drawn into the bushes, until the leaves fairly quivered with it. Birds flew near and gently perched on its notes. Other creatures sat still and silent and listened. The forest was being blessed; it was Marika singing. But now, the music was emanating from beneath the ground.

Soon after moving to her new underground quarters for the remainder of the winter, Marika had discovered that singing in this maze of habitats had a most unusual effect. Somehow the music floated out and down and through and around all the many chambers that connected her suite of rooms to those of the Fairies. It then echoed back, carrying with it the sweet, bell-like voices of a hundred spirits as they, themselves, sang and gossiped and laughed with one another. It was the magical sound of community; intertwined lives and shared being; a community in perfect harmony.

"So this is why they coaxed and prodded me here," Marika would often think to herself. "To have me be experiencing this mutual blessing for myself. Not for my body's safety and comfort alone, but for the comfort of my heart, the safety of my soul," she realized. And she loved these beings all the more for it.

It had not been an easy thing – the moving of her underground. To begin with, there had been the challenge of teaching her how to enter on her own. First, she was shown to the base of a most unremarkable fallen pine tree, practically identical looking to a thousand others in the forest. But a precise arrangement of pinecones at the entrance acted as an identifier. The scent, she knew, would become her own over time. Then, Cian and Wee Ann worked with her for hours and hours, grasping either side of her by the arms, bringing her underground without so much as the dislodging of a single pebble or the disturbance of a tiny root hair. They stepped forward, took a slight hop up and out ever so gently, and they were neatly and precisely inside. Back they would take her to the surface and repeat the procedure over and over again.

"You see, it's more a matter of how you think than who you are. It's in your mind more than your body," Cian would try to explain. "You *believe* you can do it, and there you are." He made it sound quite simple.

At last, Marika felt ready to try it on her own, and found her skirt completely tangled in the roots that veiled the entrance, her feet nowhere near where they should be, and her knickers in an unmerciful state.

"That wasn't quite right, was it?" she said looking at Cian with chagrin.

"Hmmm. Are you in?" he asked.

"As you can see, not completely."

"Then, as you say … it *wasn't quite right.* Nor was it anywhere *near* right. No one has ever been *less* right. If being right was…"

"Perhaps you could give me a hand," she interrupted, as she struggled to free herself.

"You just have to *think* your way in," he said again with as much patience as he could muster while he helped pull her from her wedge. "Forget about where you are, forget about size, and just ... leap!"

"Think in," Wee Ann echoed with a hopeful smile. "Faith!"

With the next attempt, Marika progressed substantially farther, but then her shoulders got lodged in the web of roots and dirt flew everywhere.

"Well, if you're going to widen the opening like that every time you enter, you might as well just bring a shovel and be done with it," Cian mocked. "We could even hang out a shingle over it saying: Marika's secret hiding place, everybody welcome."

Marika snorted dirt out of her nose and shook her hair and skirts, dislodged her left shoe, and prepared to try again.

Conrí, who had been watching quietly, but with obvious fascination during the entire morning's trials, sauntered over to the opening, sniffed it thoroughly, and jumped down it head first. The lively bark that followed indicated his success.

"The dog makes it on the first try," Cian smirked.

"Try again," Wee Ann encouraged. "This time, for sure!"

Marika smiled her appreciation, closed her eyes, focused her entire being on her thoughts, and imagined herself through the entrance. "Now, if I can just do that for real," she thought as she opened her eyes. And, lo and behold, she was already in.

"I did it!" she called up with excitement. "I well and truly did it!"

"You don't say," Cian spoke back. "The fact that we don't see you up here gave us that impression as well. "

Wee Ann was clapping her approval.

"And, by the way," Cian continued, "when you're underground, you don't have to shout. We can hear you quite well when you speak normally."

"How do I get back out," Marika said with a sudden thought and a bit of anxiousness.

"Same way ... in reverse," Cian said from above.

"Think up. Jump," Wee Ann added helpfully.

Thankfully, Marika was successful at exiting on the first try, despite a bit of a rocky landing, face down in the grass.

Cian laughed heartily, but pulled her to her feet. "You'll do," he said. "It will come," he finished with a sudden show of kindness, for which Marika was duly thankful. By the time she was upright, Conrí was already standing calmly at her side, tail wagging. She wrinkled her nose at him, but he chose not to see it.

The next hurdle she faced for underground living was to rearrange the space given to her. It was, after all, temporary accommodations – just until the end of her year of decision, and that would be concluding in only a few more months now; a time fast-approaching, in the middle of spring.

The space that had been granted to her was within an existing sort of storage and archive suite. There were casks of fermenting ales and wines, boxes of dried grains, and bundles of rolled leaves; all of which she carefully realigned against one wall. In a small alcove, many herbs and flowers and grasses were drying overhead, hanging in neat bunches and bouquets. The air throughout her apartment was thus delightfully spiced and fragranced, to her great delight.

Along another wall, there were stacks and rows of books and bound papers and a lovely, large writing desk with long quill pens and wells of rich inks of every color. Marika enjoyed this part of her rooms the best and left things exactly as they were. She would often spend hours on end browsing through the stored knowledge to which she had been bestowed complete and unrestricted access.

Many of the papers she found were brown with time and had

crackled edges and smelled of the ages. Marika could only imagine the centuries of wisdom and history they preserved. Some of the archived treasures that she read told of kings and queens and scores of places the Fairies had traveled to and experienced while living openly within the world, among the "others." They recorded a few alliances and feasts and friendships; but mostly, they recounted conflicts and wars, famines and harsh rations, and spoke of the cruelty and degradation they had withstood before the time of their leaving.

She was particularly intrigued to find that visitors like she were rare, and that generation after generation would pass with no mention of even the slightest contact with outsiders. And with that discovery, she felt the privilege of her status even more keenly, with even deeper gratitude.

It was in a corner near to this "library" that Marika recreated her sleeping pallet of pinestraw. A small quilt she had found airing on an unattended porch during one of her excursions into town made the small bed perfectly cozy and warm. Danny's jacket still supplied a dear pillow for her head. Next to the entrance, she created a smaller bed of straw for Conrí, which he methodically rearranged and fluffed and perfected every night before he circled and curled into position.

Most nights, she ate her evening meal in the company of Fairies; often above ground, seated on smooth, wide stones around an open campfire. Their chatter and laughter was as warming to her heart as the cooking fire was to her outstretched toes. Other times, she cooked for herself on a small open fire that she would build in the center of one of her underground rooms. Directly above the fire circle of stones and mud in this room, there was a small opening to the outside. Passersby might see only an unassuming mouse or mole hole – or the entrance to the home of any number of creatures who burrow beneath the surface of the ground. Just the occasional curl of smoke that arose while she prepared a fish or roasted some chestnuts would belie the real purpose of the opening. But here, tucked safely within the center of the enchanted forest, near the Carolina Bay itself, outside eyes were not likely to have a chance to glimpse even that telltale sign.

There was, of course, unimagined magic in the Fairies' underground dwellings, she discovered. For one thing, there was the relevance of size. Things were what they were above ground, and became what they needed to be when brought below. Her clothes continued to fit (the red sweater from Maggie remaining its own exception) no matter where she happened to be; dishes and cups and other conveniences were the perfect size underground just as they were above. Even Conrí stood, at his shoulder, a height that reached to Marika's hip, his head at her waist – regardless of whether they were above or below the ground. The Fairies themselves continued to fade and grow, shrink and dissolve, seemingly at will. But they appeared to do it more readily in the above ground world than when they were below. It was one part of their magic about which Marika sensed she should not ask – nor would they have answered, truth be told.

Another lovely magical intrigue Marika beheld was the lighting of the spaces below ground. She noticed that from early morning until late at night, she had the perfect light for whatever her task. There were no dark corners. There was no difficulty in reading letters or drawing pictures or mending a hem at any time of day or night. Nor was there ever a need to burn a candle to see one's way into bed. At first – being a girl of practical ingenuity – she believed this to be a planned architectural alignment between the underground living entrances and the track of the sun overhead. But she learned quite quickly that such an arrangement simply could not be the case. As an example, she observed, well after the sun had set and the shadows were at their deepest in the world above, she had the ideal light at her shoulder for reading in her bed below (a favorite nightly pastime). And yet, as soon as her eyes began drifting shut, and the book was sliding to her side, the light would dim itself into nothingness, and only the moon was left to peek in on her through the night. She made a note on a scrap of paper one dark afternoon to ask Cian or one of the others about this wonderful convenience.

Soon after her arrival, she had also noted the amazing artistry of the Fairies, especially as it was applied to their underground quarters. She had only glimpses of it at first – during her assisted escapes from Jacko's chases. But when her underground relocation was complete, she had plenty of time (and lighting) to study the remarkable works. She discovered that throughout the vast underground maze of rooms and passages, on the plain dirt walls and floors and ceilings and every space imaginable, there were wondrous works of elaborate, pristine, perfectly executed art, in a rainbow of colors and shades and hues. Some were like oil paintings; some of pastels; there were watercolors and pen-and-ink and charcoal. Some were more like carvings and mosaics that were as beautiful to the touch as they were to the eye. And one *could* touch any of the marvelous works of art and walk on them and lean against them, even wash and brush them, and move spider webs away from their centers to unused corners, and the images never smudged nor dimmed in the least.

Marika was marveling at one particularly intricate and captivating scene on the ceiling of a passageway one day when a Fairy she had seen but never met came and stood next to her. For a long moment, the Fairy leaned his head far back and studied the mural along with Marika.

"Do you like it?" he asked frankly.

"Oh yes," Marika responded with a respectful sigh.

"Hmm. Could be better. Could be better," he critiqued.

"Oh, no – do you think so? I believe it is just the loveliest thing I've ever seen." It was a pastoral scene, in the style of the European masters, and Marika was partial to this type of art.

"Still, it needs freshening at least," the Fairy said. And with that, he waved his arm over his head and hissed a sort of rush of air through his teeth – and the beautiful mural had disappeared entirely.

Marika was devastated, and a bit angry. "What have you done? Why have you destroyed it?" she asked with passion. And then, upon more thought: "*How* did you do that?"

"It was my work, you see," he stated. "Only I have the power to keep or remove my own work. And I chose to remove this one. I'll redo it – don't worry. You'll like the revision even more ... promise!" He gave her a wink and then set to work on a completely fresh canvas. "Come back in a few days. You'll see."

But perhaps the most perplexing of all the unique aspects and nuances of the Fairy world was the absence of any Fairy babies or very young ones. The only exception to this were the Water Babies (who have a history all their own). Marika had been told about this phenomenon by her Gran during their many walks in the forest, but she had now had it proved to her throughout her stay, and confirmed absolutely with her move underground.

In some of the ancient literature she found in the archives, she read about Fairies being "created" in numerous and varied ways. With very few exceptions, she learned, they come into being fully grown and never age. What she had not known, however, is that each chooses for himself or herself the talents they want to possess upon the anniversary of their thirteenth year on earth – and they must abide by that decision for at least the next century.

Yet in other obscure references, the girl found it was said that new Fairies come into being riding on the breath of the first soft laughter of a newborn babe. And then, in still less seen passages it was written that a human child must only "believe" to create a new life among the world of the Fae. And one rainy afternoon, tucked inside the pages of one exceedingly thick volume of stories, Marika unfolded a note claiming that, with every original tale told, an original Fairy is born. Marika quite frankly did not know which of these historical documents to believe – perhaps a bit of them all, she finally reasoned, as she had learned even in her short life that the truth is rarely completely one thing or another, but rather dependent on one's point of view.

And so, Marika spent much of the winter reading and listening, studying and learning the ways of the Fairy society, absorbing their history and culture, deepening the bonds she felt with them, and experiencing a sense of security and belonging that was more real and complete than anything she had known throughout most of her young life.

Deep in January, Marika was brought back into the uncompromising embrace of the outside world once again.

"Marika ... ," the voice whispered in the night. The girl stirred awake. She wasn't at all certain if she had heard this sound or if she had dreamed it into her ears.

But there, standing in the far corner of the room, with moonlight reflecting halos from her hair and robes, was Saoirse, the Fairy whose name was Freedom.

The spirit did not speak again, but motioned to Marika to follow her. She dissolved into a silver mist that floated and wafted out the tree-root entrance of Marika's quarters, and then re-formed into her being a few yards away.

Marika quickly pulled her shoes on in the dim light and followed her friend. Conrí was at her heels.

"Where are we going, Saoirse?" Marika asked just loudly enough for the Fairy to hear. But there was no answer. Saoirse remained at least ten feet in front of the girl and her dog. She never even turned to see if they followed.

The wintry mist was low and chill and dampened Marika's skirts and shoes to her skin. She shivered slightly as she watched Saoirse seemingly float across the ground, fading and glowing in the moon-dappled shadows that surrounded them. There was an almost unnatural hush to the fog. It silenced their footfalls and drank in their breath.

"Saoirse," Marika spoke in whispers still. "Please tell me where you are leading me. Where are we going?"

Saoirse turned then, and looked at the girl, but did not speak. Marika could not see her face clearly. But she had great faith in this Fairy who had twice saved her from Jacko. Saoirse was always more aloof than the others. But Marika felt safe with her and knew that, of all the Fairies of the gathering, she was among the most respected. And so, she followed in quiet obedience.

They traveled out of the forest, down roads with which Marika was not immediately familiar. They passed the plantation of Isaac Winston. Marika shuddered at the memory and quickened her steps. Even in the mist and haze and soft light of the moon, Marika could see the degrading splendor of the place – the declining opulence.

Not far after they had passed the fences marking the outer edge of the plantation, Saoirse stopped. She turned to Marika and put her finger across the shadow of her lips signaling silence. She bent low and crept on her hands and knees beneath low-hanging branches of cypress trees and pines and weeping willows. Marika followed, with Conrí right behind. There was not a sound from any of them.

Slowly, Marika became aware of campfires ahead. The firelight was half encircled by covered wagons, the sight of which brought memories to the surface of her heart in a cold, harsh rush. A *thribli*. Jacko's *thribli*! There was no other in this part of the world, she knew.

Marika wanted to flee. But Saoirse's hand gripped her wrist – and it was warm and comforting, reassuring. Her heart slowed its fluttering, and she was able to see and hear clearly again. The fires crackled. A few unseen men laughed at some unheard joke; one of them began to wheeze and choke on the end of it; an uncouth spit landed in the fire.

Marika focused her mind and listened deeply. Closer to them, another man was singing. It was soft and low – a black man's spiritual, sung with a black man's understanding. But something else, as well: the sound of a man who has lost all hope.

"Ishmael?" Marika wondered to herself.

Saoirse nodded as if the girl had spoken out loud to her.

Ishmael, here? Yes! Jacko's words that night in the woods now echoed in her ears: *"Now you belong to me."*

But what did Saoirse want of her? Why had she brought her here?

Before her eyes could even question Saoirse, the singing man began to approach them. Ishmael was coming near them with a bucket of dirty water, ready to cast it into the woods. He walked an unsteady, stumbling gate – with a slight limp and hop. His hands shook. He picked at his worn, thin shirt with the anxious fingers of his right hand, while the bucket of water sloshed in his left.

Marika turned to look at Saoirse for direction, but the Fairy had disappeared. The girl was there alone. And Ishmael was quickly closing the gap between them. He was reciting nonsensical words and rhymes. Spittle formed in bubbles at the corners of his mouth. His nose ran unheeded. His mind was gone, Marika could well see.

Without thought, Marika began to sing as well – very quietly, very low. She sang as she had sung to Ishmael in the cabin where Joseph had treated the slave's wounds months ago. Ishmael stopped suddenly. He listened acutely. And Marika saw one silent tear streak his unwashed black cheek.

"I was with Joseph, Ishmael," she whispered. "Do you remember? My name is Marika."

"I remembers," Ishmael said at last, as quietly as she. He looked over his shoulder, his eyes sweeping the encampment. He twitched and dropped the pail. Then he sang his tune a bit more, and somewhat loudly.

"Why is you here?" he asked as he turned back to the darkness. "Where is you? Is you jes' a voice in ma' head?"

"Here, Ishmael. I'm real. I'm here," Marika whispered back and she cautiously stood up so he could see her.

"Why does you come here? Why is you here? Why is you here? Why is you here?" he said over and over because he could not stop.

"I don't know," Marika interrupted and answered frankly. "A friend of mine brought me to you."

The man's eyes darted back and forth, across the darkness; suddenly, they fluttered back into his head, and Marika was afraid he was going to fall. "She's gone now," she assured him. "It's only me and Conrí – the dog."

"What name is you? What name? What name?" Ishmael stuttered again and again, faster and faster.

"Marika! My name is Marika. I'm a friend of Joseph's," she started to explain again.

"I know. I know. I know. I know. Marika. Marika. Marika. I

hear men talk that name. Mista Jacko. Mista Jacko. He my massah now. He talks your name. I remember. Marika. That name. Mista Jacko." Ishmael was terribly agitated and his body was twitching violently, as the words came tumbling out.

Marika turned ice inside. But she had to find out. "What does he say about me, Ishmael? Please tell me."

"Jacko look for Marika. Oh, yeah. Marika belong to Jacko, oh yessir. He gonna find you, fo' sure. He gonna find you good!" Ishmael released a pent up sob and a laugh all at once. Then he hung his head on his chest.

"He got ugly thoughts. Ugly heart," he said.

"Does he say anything else?" Marika pushed, knowing she needed to hear.

"He curse you. He curse a man he call your 'Da.' Dishonor, he say. Shame, he say."

Marika could no longer feel her legs or the cold air or mist or fear. "He wears a long green scarf, Ishmael. Has ever he said where he got that scarf?"

Ishmael felt the girl's passion and need across the darkness that separated them. He must say the truth to her, he knew. And something almost forgotten inside of him strengthened him and cleared his thoughts for that one fleeting moment. "He say he got it from a dead man's throat. Took it from him hisself."

Ishmael looked at the girl with clarity of sight and mind. "I's sorry, Miss. Too, too, sorry."

Marika was absolutely silent. A calmness took over her, steadied her soul, assured her of a truth she had refused to admit into her heart for months. She knew he was gone. Had known for a long time. Sometime last spring, she thought. Not long after she had last seen him. To what extent Jacko had participated in his death, she did not know. But he had been there, that was certain. Da was gone.

The clarity in Ishmael's eyes began to fade, then. He stuttered and recited and drooled his nonsense again. He picked at his sleeves and pulled out large twists of his hair until his scalp bled. He turned to leave and return to the camp.

"Wait," Marika called out to him faintly but firmly. "Ishmael – wait."

He stopped where he stood and did not turn toward her.

"Do you want to be free, Ishmael?" she asked in a flat tone but with a sudden and deep understanding.

He stood, silent, for a long moment. "Yes," he said huskily and with complete comprehension.

THE TRIAL.

The seasons walked on cat paws out of winter into early spring. Softly, unnoticed, it was just gently there one particular morning. The pre-dawn praise by the songbirds of the forest had just begun. The first few fluttering notes floated on the early mists, cajoling others to wake and rejoice and sing up the sun.

Marika stirred. Not fully asleep, not fully awake, she snuggled deeply into the soft, downy comfort of the moment.

Her ears noticed the sudden silence well before her mind grasped its significance.

She breathed in the scented early spring and tasted its promises. New blossoms and fresh shades of green were painted across the woodlands every day now. Every morning walk was a re-born pleasure to her senses and soul.

Perhaps it was nearby thunder that rumbled – a spring shower being announced. No, not quite. Her consciousness was alerted. It was the sound of running. Fast, fearful running. Human.

Marika sat upright with absolute awareness. She hurried to the entrance of her below-ground dwelling and listened intently as she pulled on her clothing and shoes. She detected hounds baying on scent.

Conrí was already waiting for her above ground. He was leaning into the sound – the chase – muscles tensed, head tilting to discern the origin of it. It was somewhere just beyond the edge, the other side of the veil, but near.

Marika could hear the labored, fearful breathing of the hunted. She sensed the stumbles and falls, the motivating terror.

She cautiously made her way to the secret gates and listened in silence. The hounds could still be heard, but now at least half a mile away, she judged.

One step forward ... another. She passed through the veil, keeping Conrí at her heel. She felt a presence, but saw no one. A bird flew with alarm from a nearby bush, followed by a soft sob escaping an unwilling throat.

"It's all right. The hounds have passed," Marika whispered in the direction of the hidden cry. "It's safe," she reassured.

Slowly, Caleb crawled free of the brush where he was hiding. He looked first at Marika, then Conrí, then scanned the forest as far as he could see in every direction. His body was rigid with fear.

"Hello, Caleb," Marika said softly. "Do you remember me? I'm a friend of Joseph."

"Yes, Miss. I remembers." His voice shook as he sank to the ground to sit and recover his breathing and strength.

"What were you running from?" Marika questioned. "Who was chasing you? Why?"

"We was caught," Caleb answered looking up at her through a sideways glance. His head hung against his chest.

"Caught where? Doing what?" Marika prodded.

"Readin' and writin', Miss. It was at Miss Maggie's place. She learns us to read – at night. But this time they came up on us quick as lightnin' – quick as anything you done seen. Musta been waitin' for us. Somebody musta know'd we'd be there." He shook his head slowly, as if to clear the fear from it, to better grasp what had just happened.

He continued: "Miss Maggie ... she tol' us to run – run fast – into the woods, she says. They was grabin' at us and grabin' at us – but she kep' stepping' up and holdin' on to 'em. There was three, mebbe four of 'em. And hounds! They set the hounds to us soon as we run out the door."

Caleb stopped to catch his breath and Marika sat down next to him on the ground. She put her arm gently around his shoulders and patted him with her hand. Involuntarily, he jerked from the innocent touch. But then he looked in her face, and let her arm remain across his back. She stayed quiet, letting him tell her in his own time, but her stomach lurched and her heart pounded – wondering, knowing.

"Most of us got to the woods and kep' a runnin' – through the water and brush – all different ways – jes' like Miss Maggie said to do. But the hounds done found jes' 'bout ever las' one of us. I saw 'em catch my mama." Caleb stopped with a quivering intake of breath then, and Marika wiped at his tears with one of her sleeves. But still, she remained silent and listened.

"I don't know what happened to th' others. But I knows they catched my mama, and they was a holdin' on to Miss Maggie, and everybody jes' run like the devil," he concluded.

"How many of you were there?" Marika asked then.

"There was seven of us – and Miss Maggie," he answered.

"What will happen next, Caleb?" Marika spoke with anxiousness.

"Whippin's mostly," Caleb shivered. "Whippin's for the black folks, and paying money for Miss Maggie, mos' likely."

"Will they whip Miss Maggie? Or put her in jail?" Marika questioned, unsure of the law and custom here.

"Prob'ly not," Caleb shook his head thinking. Then his soft brown eyes welled up and overflowed in hot, bitter tears. "But they's gonna whip mama fo' sure. We been caught before. They's gonna whip mama." Caleb laid his young head on his arms across his knees and wept for his mother's anticipated humiliation and pain. Marika cried with him.

Several minutes passed while the two young people helplessly grieved and shared their fear.

Suddenly, Marika's head snapped up.

"Hush," she cautioned Caleb. A lone horse was approaching.

"Hide!" she hissed to him, as she began to push him toward the tangled brush that surrounded them.

"Marika," a familiar voice called out. "Is that you, Child?" Joseph's welcome presence came into view.

"Oh, Joseph," both children echoed with deep heart-felt relief.

Marika stood and pulled Caleb up with her.

"Help us, Joseph. You've got to help Caleb and his mama – and Miss Maggie," she pleaded before Joseph was able to even dismount from his horse. The man's face revealed that he knew of the discovery and capture. He understood.

"First of all, I'm going to take Caleb to Doc's house," Joseph told them decisively. "No one can prove he hasn't been there all night and Doc will swear to it. No one can prove he was anywhere near Maggie's place. Do you understand, Caleb?" he said as he turned and leaned down to look the boy in his eyes. "You were helping wash-up medicine bottles and it got late and you stayed the night – you understand?"

"Yessir," Caleb responded.

"Good. After that, I'll go over to the Magistrate's and see what I can find out about the others," he continued.

Marika beseeched him with her eyes.

"Including Miss Maggie," Joseph assured her.

He swung Caleb into the saddle and pulled himself up behind

him. He held the horse in check and said to Marika: "It's going to be all right, Child."

"No it isn't," she said back with a depth of comprehension he hadn't expected.

"No ... it isn't," he replied truthfully to her. "But Doc will help. And so will the rest of the Quakers. We'll do all we can. I promise you that, Child."

"Yes, Joseph," she replied.

She called out softly as they turned to ride away: "*Go bhfóire Dia orthu!* (God help them!)"

Days passed with no word from Joseph.

Marika ventured into town on several occasions to find out what she could for herself. Between alleyways and beneath open windows, behind shirts and trousers drying in side yards, and at the open market in the square, to say nothing of just outside the smoky doorway of the pub at the end of Main Street, the story came to her in bits and pieces. It was a topic on every tongue. And everyone had an opinion.

"I must say, Isaac Winston is making a right fuss over it all."

"Well, it was mostly his black folks involved. Can't say he don't have a right to fuss."

"What was Miss Maggie thinking? A fine woman, I ain't saying she's not. But – bless her heart – what *was* she thinking? It's not like she hasn't been warned before."

"Bold as brass, she can be at times. Bold as brass!"

"She needs a man to keep her in her place is what I think."

"Mmmm. It's that Quaker nonsense that brings her to it – *everybody's equal in the eyes of the Lord* ..."

"It's a dangerous thing for slaves to be able to read and write, anyway. Dangerous thing!"

"What's the Magistrate gonna do, is what I wonder."

"Whipping, I 'spect. Don't much like it myself, of course. But how else are they gonna learn? And the law's the law."

"Magistrate Jones is gonna take it on."

"Oh Lordy. Reverend Jones? You know he's gonna take it for all it's worth, you just know that."

"That man's a little king just looking for a throne! Fair, mind you, but looking for a throne."

"Well, I heard Isaac Winston was plumb out of money – in spite of that big ol' plantation. You can see how he's just let it go all down hill. He lost it all, gaming and horses and women and such. Like as not he'll be looking to get what he can out of this mess."

"You know he already lost Ishmael. He ain't got much left in the way of slave stock. Mostly women and them that's too young or too old."

"He'll be cashin' in on this for sure."

"Poor Miss Maggie!"

"What's she gonna do?"

"Looking to get what he can ..."

"Plenty of whippings ..."

"The law's the law ..."

The words tumbled over and over through Marika's head, and she ran as fast as her legs would move her away from town. Across the fields, into the forest, splashing through the streams. She ran and ran and ran all the harder to make the blood pound in her ears, to beat down the voices. She ran until she got a sharp catch in her side and had to collapse on the ground, her breath jagged and heaving. Conrí barely kept up, his tongue hanging long from the side of his gaping mouth.

She rolled onto her stomach and crawled to the nearby edge of the stream to drink and cool her face. Conrí was already quenching his thirst in its clear, eddying pools.

The sun was streaking through the giant columns of trees on long, thin fingers. The shadows seemed almost black against its brilliance. She faced the gently moving water and cupped and dipped her hands into its clear, refreshing liquid. A thick green leaf floated in front of her and caught on a gray river rock just at the water's edge. Pushing it away, she watched the reflections of the tree tops swaying in the breeze above her, and remembered her first encounter last year at just this time with Cian, her first touch with the Fairy world and all its enchantments. It calmed her thoughts, as she recalled how she had seen his face so clearly in the water next to hers – and the clouds and trees as they bowed and floated past, behind her own reflection. But now ... now, she found her own image was somehow blurred and faint – hardly there at all!

She ran the palm of her hand across the surface of the pool to try to clear it; she shifted her position to block the sun a bit more. It was unmistakable. Her image was faded. She pulled away quickly, and leaned far back from the water's edge. She stood on unsure legs, and began walking with purpose toward the enchanted part of the forest. By the time she reached the gates, she was almost running. She leaped through the opening with Conrí close behind, and let it close tightly behind them. And, immediately, she went in search of explanation and comfort – some words and reason to soothe her fears.

The stars were early rising that night; a dark moon gave them an empty stage upon which to dance and sparkle in their finery and perform their visual magic. On the forest floor below, Marika had joined the Fairies around a campfire and a fine dinner of early spring sprouts and tender shoots and fresh-caught fish. But she only picked around the edges of the food, as she picked around the edges of her questions.

"Cian," she began to her friend at her side, "I've noticed something that I can't explain."

"Just one thing? I notice at least ten things everyday that I would imagine you couldn't explain," he teased.

"Cian."

"Sorry, my dear. What is bothering you?"

She took a deep breath: "Can you see me?"

Cian snickered at first, but then saw her face and became serious again.

"Yes. Can you see me?" he answered.

"I mean, can you see me clearly? Am I faint looking? Can you see me just like always? Do I have colors and form and, and – can you just see me like always?" she finished in a near whisper of frustration and fear.

"Ah!" Cian replied with sudden understanding. "Have you noticed your image getting less clear and defined when you look into the waters over the past several days?"

"Oh, yes," she breathed with relief that it was real and not her imagination, and that Cian would know the cause. "Actually, I just noticed it today – in the forest outside the gates."

"Your time is getting near, Luv, that's all. Your year of decision is drawing to a close. But surely you knew that. You could feel it inside you, now, couldn't you?"

"Yes, I suppose I did," Marika answered honestly. "But with so many other things happening ... I suppose I hadn't taken notice. I'm sorry – I should have. I won't forget my pledge, my promise," she said solemnly.

"We know," Cian responded.

It was then that Marika realized all of the other Fairies in the gathering had become uncharacteristically quiet. They were quite blatantly listening to what she and Cian were discussing.

"We want you. Stay, please." It was Wee Ann who spoke first.

"Hush," Cian cautioned her. "Her decision will be her own."

"Aye, aye," the other Fairies agreed. But they watched her with eyes that spoke more clearly than their words ever could.

The silence continued as all ate quietly with their own thoughts.

"What will happen if I won't be choosing to stay?" Marika then asked with a tightness in her throat that she couldn't swallow away.

"Your image will become fainter and fainter here in the enchanted part of the forest. You won't be able to see us as clearly either. You will lose your ability to go to your underground quarters. Then, on the stroke of midnight on the last day of your year, you will no longer belong to the forest. The gates will have disappeared. The veil will no longer exist. And that night you will sleep, and when you awake, you will have only the vaguest of memories of us or this place or your life among us. Some things you will forget altogether. All of this will be lost to you." Cian spoke with no inflection, just stating these things in factual terms. But it wrapped Marika with a cold chill she could not escape even as she inched closer to the fire, and her heart filled with a deep, sad loneliness.

None of the other Fairies spoke a word or made a sound.

"And what will it be like if I will be choosing this world over that of the others? What will happen if I am wanting to stay with you?" Marika asked as well.

Cian responded in a similar unemotional, controlled fashion: "Your image will become fainter in the outside world, and stronger here among us. You will be able to hear less clearly the sounds from the other side of the veil. Your powers of magic will become stronger; but you will be expected to control them absolutely. You will be able to venture into the outside among the others at will. But you will be unseen by them. They and their world will change and grow old and die and move on. But you will stay forever as you are now. Soon, you will find you no longer want to walk among them. You will forget all but the strongest ties and emotions you had with the others. And they will have forgotten you completely. You will become like a dream barely remembered to that world – a secret forgotten."

Marika sucked in her breath; images of Joseph and Maggie and Caleb and her *thribli* all filled her eyes. And she realized, perhaps for the first time, that she would be choosing between two absolutes. This year of living in and between both worlds had been an uncommon privilege, and it would soon be gone forever. She had been living "in" both worlds, but not "of" either of them.

"The price of freedom to choose is dear, is it not?" Cian said then with finality.

The fire crackled loudly as a log fell heavily into the embers and sparks jumped and rushed and pushed each other along the up-drafts into the sky. It broke the spell of silence, and the Fairies began to chatter and laugh again. Cian moved away. The evening continued with unnatural normalcy.

The tentative calls of the early morning birds awoke her; and on the gentle warm breeze of the pink and yellow dawn, Marika arose and began to dress carefully to go into town. She had slept little and fitfully. This was the day of the trial for Maggie and the captured slaves.

It took her three tries before she could achieve her assent from her below-ground dwelling place. Tonight, she thought to herself, she must reclaim her old home at the edge of the Bay.

For the first time since they had found each other, Marika

commanded Conrí to wait at the gates of the forest, forbidding him to follow her. He obeyed with great disgust and little understanding. He "hurumphed" himself down on the ground at the base of a tree.

As Marika walked the back roads toward town, she noted the increase in traffic. Men and women and families, on foot and in wagons and carriages, all were traveling in the direction of Maggie's farm, where the court was to be held. The Magistrate had rightly judged the interest of the community, and realized more onlookers could be accommodated at her place than in town, where he typically held his hearings from the porch of the general store. And Reverend Jones was nothing if not accommodating to those who wished to visit his court, and be an audience for the performance of his duties.

Marika felt ill and faint, but walked steadily and mingled unseen among the others to the edge of the farm. Most of the crowd had brought blankets and small pillows for sitting comfortably on the ground. They all politely preempted each other for the choicest spots. Marika fell back to the outer edge of the gathering, then climbed a nearby flowering pear tree to hear and watch unnoticed. She clung to its sturdy limbs, curtained by its leafy branches and remaining white blossoms, and gratefully took in its familiar nutty scent.

From her vantage point, Marika could see Maggie seated on the porch. She was in one of her own kitchen chairs a few feet from where the Magistrate would preside. Her hands were constantly moving in her lap, pulling and plucking at a small white handkerchief. Occasionally, she would dab at her mouth and upper lip with the lace-edged bit of cloth. But her back was straight and her chin high. And, from time to time, she would turn and smile and nod reassuringly to the row of six black women and children that stood behind her. Marika could not make out the quiet words she was speaking to them, but she watched her with a feeling of pride.

The Magistrate had ordered two men to carry Maggie's thick oak kitchen table onto the front porch for him to use as his legal bench. Marika thought back to the first dinner Maggie had shared with her at that table, and it outraged her to see it now being used for such a purpose. It had been a place of hospitality, of welcoming warmth to a frightened, grieving young girl. And now it was being used in the judgment of the very woman who owned it.

Seated at the end of a row of chairs facing the Magistrate's bench was Doc Jackson. He was watching Maggie with close attention and a professional eye. His jaw flexed constantly, although he was leaning back in the chair with seeming confidence.

At the other end of the same row sat Isaac Winston. He was dressed in what had been his finest attire. But now it was soiled and stained and sorely in need of a good pressing. His cuffs were worn and his boots scuffed. He crossed his left leg over his right one, and Marika could see great holes in the bottom of his sole. Across his cheeks and chin was an uneven stubble. His hands shook, and he tried to hide them in his pockets. His feet never stopped moving, the toes of his right foot lifting his knee in a constant bounce.

Joseph stood not far away, but off to the side, at the edge of the crowd. He held onto Caleb's tightly balled fist, and patted the boy's back with his other large, comforting hand. Marika wanted to run to them, too, but knew she must not.

The Magistrate, Reverend Jones, was a physically small man. Not much taller than herself, Marika's eye measured. But, rather predictably, what he lacked in stature, he assumed in attitude. He strutted across the porch to the chair placed behind the square oak kitchen table, ready to take charge and begin the proceedings. He sat down and all but disappeared. Only his round red face and balding head peeked above the table's mass. A few snorts and twitters of laughter fluttered across the crowd. Even Maggie's mouth twitched at the corners. He stood up again immediately, and gruffly called for a taller stool to be brought to him. Maggie graciously told a man where one could be found inside her house.

With the stool in place, cautiously tried and found satisfactory by the Reverend Jones himself, he pulled a very large mallet from his coat pocket, and banged the crowd into silence, and the court into order.

His voice boomed, belying his small size, and Marika could well imagine his presence in a church setting. He would be one to go on for hours and hours, she sighed. But she kept remembering one phrase she had heard in town: "... a fair man." She prayed with all her heart that he would bring his sense of justice to this day.

"Mrs. Magdalena Nydegger," the Magistrate began in an officious tone, "charges have been brought against you for violating the law and instructing a number of slaves to read and write; that number being three Negro female adults and three Negro boys. Furthermore, that these Negro slaves are not your property but belong to one Isaac Winston, a free black man and property owner in this county." He cleared his throat and looked at Maggie then; Marika thought his face softened just a bit.

"Is that about the size of it Miss Nydegger?" he concluded.

Maggie nodded her head and rose to speak. "Yes, Robert – ah – Reverend Jones – Magistrate. I do not deny those charges against me."

"She's ruined my people!" Isaac had risen, too, and shouted from the front row. "Jes' plain ruined 'em for any kind a field work. Too high and mighty once they gets to reading. Jes' ruined 'em!" He had knocked over his chair and was stumbling to grasp the one next to it. "An' there's one missing from that porch, Mr. Magistrate. That boy

Caleb was one of 'em. Swear to God he was one of 'em.'"

"Sit down, Mr. Winston," the Magistrate said as he banged his gavel to also quiet the crowd. "You'll have your chance to speak when I tell you." He pounded the table and repeated, "Sit down!"

Someone had righted the overturned chair and Isaac resumed his seat. His arms were folded across his chest defiantly.

The Magistrate referred to some notes he had taken out of his pocket and placed in front of him. He raised his eyes to Maggie's face. "Now then, Miss Nydegger, you are owning to the charge of teaching the Negro property of another citizen to read and write, and doing so in secrecy and under the dark of night?"

Maggie drew her hands into fists, but kept them at her sides. Her voice was well controlled: "I plead guilty to teaching six *human beings* to read and write in the privacy of my home. I also want to point out that these individuals are relations of Mr. Isaac Winston, including his sister, his sister-in-law and her sister, and a few of their sons. While it's true that Mr. Winston bought these relatives from their former bondage – although he has not yet seen fit to free them of his own accord – it would seem to me that, as a freed man himself, Mr. Winston might be more in favor of improving the lives of his own people. It would seem to me that he would want them to be able to read and write and do sums and be a contributing part of his farm – not just to be used for pure strong-backed labor!" Her breathing was coming fast and her color was high, but Maggie kept her temper and her grace.

Doc was smiling ear to ear, as were many others present. But Isaac scowled and glowered behind his still-folded arms.

The Magistrate banged the gavel and stared hard at Maggie himself. "Miss Nydegger, it is *against the law* to teach slaves to read and write – it don't matter what the owner wants and don't want. And it sure don't matter what a neighbor thinks is right or ought to be. The law's the law! You do understand that, I trust."

"Yes, Magistrate," Maggie answered calmly. "Of that charge, I am guilty, as I have said." Her chin was high and the crowd discussed it thoroughly.

The gavel banged. Isaac arranged himself on his chair with obvious satisfaction. Maggie stood in her place, all nervousness seemed to have left her.

The Magistrate asked Maggie to be seated. He asked Doc to stand and swear that Caleb had not been a part of the number caught in the class. Doc did as he was asked. Then the Reverend Jones invited Isaac to come to the porch and say his piece about it all.

Isaac rose and took a moment to steady himself. He walked with great deliberation and attempted dignity up the stone porch steps and stood facing the crowd. First he spit. Then he stretched out his long right arm and pointed his finger directly at Maggie. "That woman .... that woman is a-stirring up my people against me. She's a-stirring up plenty of slaves among us. You've heard the talk about the rebellion. We've all heard it. They's gonna rise up against all the landowners 'round here and they's gonna kill us all in our beds. They's gonna kill us all as we sleep! And not just the men and women … they's gonna kill our babies and young'uns. Gonna leave 'em lying in their own blood. And that woman …" (he had to practically scream to be heard over the reaction of the crowd) "…that woman is part of it all! She's teaching 'em how to read and write and how to plan the whole thing! When your sweet little girl is dying in her bed, and your innocent little boy is a-hangin' from your own apple tree, you're gonna know who to blame. *That woman!*"

Isaac was swerving dangerously close to the edge of the porch. Doc Jackson stepped up and grabbed him, as much to keep him from the fall as to restrain him from further insane outbursts. Maggie's eyes were wide with disbelief; she covered her mouth with both hands. The women behind her were crying softly and holding on to one another. The crowd was standing and yelling their own opinions to both Isaac and Maggie alike. The Magistrate was determined to gain control. He pulled up a shotgun, which he had placed at the base of the table before the proceedings had started, and blistered the air.

In an instant, the atmosphere turned from chaos to absolute silence.

"That will do, Mr. Winston," was all the Magistrate said. Doc accompanied Isaac back to his chair and seated him with firmness and a look Isaac thoroughly respected. The Reverend Jones gave a similar silent command to everyone else.

"Now that the hysterics have been completed," Magistrate Jones said to a smattering of nervous laughter, "we'll get back to this hearing.

"Miss Maggie," he began. "Are you feeling up to going on with the proceedings?"

"Yes, Magistrate, thank you."

"Then I will give you my sentence," he said with more respect and integrity than most would have credited to him at the start of the trial.

"I find you, Widow Magdalena Nydegger, guilty of the charges brought against you. I find the six Negro slaves guilty of the charges against them. I have noted that this is not the first such offense for all parties involved. And that fact has necessarily been taken into account for the sentences I am about to hand down – as has Mr. Winston's stated fear for his safety and economic wellbeing. Widow Nydegger will be fined in the amount of two-hundred dollars for each slave captured in the act of being taught to read and write. This number being six, the total fine is fixed at one-thousand-two-hundred dollars." The crowed reflected its satisfaction, but surprise at the high amount, and wondered how she might raise such a sum.

He went on, "As for the three Negro female contraband: each shall receive no less than twenty lashings in the public square. The three Negro boys shall receive ten whippings each ... with the paddle," he amended for the children. The audience again reflected agreement with the sentence. The black women wept with each other and held their young ones close. Caleb tried to escape from Joseph's loving arms, but the man wisely held him tight.

Then, Maggie stepped forward and asked if she might speak again. The Magistrate, surprised, agreed.

"Please, Reverend – Robert – please, let me offer one other solution." She turned to face Isaac. "Isaac, we've been neighbors for many, many years. We've always done right by each other. The only thing we've ever quarreled over is the issue of slavery. Trust me when I say that I have never had anything to do with any slavery uprising – any slave rebellion. I would never condone any such violence, you know that. But I tell you that in my soul I know the day is fast approaching when our country will be at war – with this very issue at the heart of it. That will be the 'rebellion,' if you want to call it that. The people will rebel – the people of this country will not tolerate this inhumane treatment of other human beings much longer. We are all God's creatures. We all must have the same rights and privileges in this nation that was built on these principles. The day is coming and it is coming soon. And all of the peoples of this country must be prepared for that future. And that begins with education – you must know that. How else can they be contributing members of our society?" Maggie had turned her attention away from Isaac and was addressing the entire crowd now, but they had become merely silent onlookers.

She faced the Magistrate again and said, "If Isaac will accept, I would like to offer to purchase these six individuals – at whatever his price – in forgiveness of their punishment." The crowd reacted then, as she swung back to Isaac, "Please, Isaac. I will pay whatever you ask. Give these people to me. Let me take them away – out west. My church is moving there. We are selling all we have here. We will take them with us, and you need not see them ever again. I will pay you in gold coins, if that's what you want. Please, Isaac, listen to me. Let this be."

She concluded by looking back at the Magistrate: "Please, sir, let this be. In your wisdom, make this decision in the name of the God we both pray to."

The Magistrate was watching Isaac, who simply nodded his head. He considered it for a moment, then, he turned to Maggie. "Let it be so ordered. The price to be paid is one-thousand dollars per slave, in addition to the twelve-hundred dollars in fines. Maggie – that's a total of seven-thousand-two-hundred dollars – to be paid in gold coins. Do you understand?"

Maggie nodded with tears blurring her vision.

"It is so ordered." The gavel banged just as an empty pear tree branch was swinging in the wind.

It was an old Irish love song. Marika's lips savored the long-remembered words with a new-found comprehension. She had always treasured the tune, as one her Da sang frequently. But the poetry of the song held new meaning for her now. It spoke of loss and long absences and sad partings. She sang it softly at the foot of Danny's grave.

The day was a blessing of nature. The air was as gentle as a Fairy's kiss. The sky was incredibly clear, near violet in color. The sun warmed Marika's shoulders and stroked the top of her head. She could almost feel Gran's touch in it.

"Oh, Danny. You would be loving this day," she whispered. "It's like heaven itself left the backdoor open. How can such a day be filled with so much sadness of the heart. But here I am, waiting for Miss Maggie to come and say goodbye to us. She did as she said, kept her word, she did. She sold off the farm and practically all she had on it, and she paid for the slaves in gold coin to Mister Isaac. So he's got his money now – his pieces of gold. But that's about all he's got. And most of that he'll be owing to the bet makers I'm thinking."

She stopped and sang a few more verses of the song for her brother. She contemplated the words again as they left her mouth. The simple, melancholy melody brought butterflies and birds near to her, and it caressed the marble and stone that surrounded them.

Marika sensed an approaching wagon, and raised her head just as Maggie was reaching the gates of the graveyard. Maggie was driving a small wood-wheeled cart that held the last of her belongings. Two horses pulled it that Marika did not recognize. The old horse and milk cow that she remembered must have been sold in auction along with all the other goods of the farm.

Seated next to Maggie on the wagon's bench was a woman of color about thirty years old. Marika saw it was Ishmael's wife – whom she had first met in the small cabin when Joseph had attended to her husband's wounds. On her lap was a small, sleeping child. Caleb was riding in the back of the wagon, atop a fat black leather trunk, with Scout the dog at his side. A few boxes and barrels of goods surrounded them. The boy looked cleaner and less anxious than anytime Marika had seen him before. He looked like someone beginning a new life, she thought to herself.

Joseph, riding on his own horse, was right behind them.

Marika stood and waved and watched them turn into the cemetery and draw near to her. She took in deep breaths to keep the tears at bay for just a bit longer.

"Marika! Child – it's so good to lay my eyes on you. I thought you would come to see me at the farm. But Joseph explained. It would have been too difficult to look at it, I know." Maggie's own tears formed new furrows down her cheeks. To Marika's eyes, her friend had aged years since the trial. What was a new beginning for Caleb, was a painfully difficult necessity to start over for Maggie.

Joseph had dismounted from his horse and came to the side of the wagon to help Maggie climb to the ground. "Have you decided?" Maggie asked of Marika before she was completely down from her wagon seat. "Are you going to come with us out west? Please, Child. It would mean so much to me to have you at my side. I know Joseph told you of my hope that you would join us. What have you decided?" Maggie's eyes were searching the ground around the grave for any trace of Marika's carpet bags – any sign that the girl was going to accompany them on their journey of relocation. "I was hoping that since you wanted to meet us here near Danny's grave, it meant you had decided to come. Was I hoping in vain?" she asked with a throb in her voice.

"I'm sorry, Miss. I cannot go," was all Marika could say. There was no explanation that would allow itself to come out of her heart. No words. "I must be staying here. But I wanted to tell you goodbye. And to be giving you something before you go."

The two friends enfolded each other in a strong and warm last embrace. Stepping back, Maggie looked deeply into Marika's eyes. "Is there no hope of your changing your mind, Child?" Maggie tried one more time. "No. I suppose not," she said with another long search of Marika's face. "You do know how much I've come to love you, don't you? You know I will always remember you – always."

Marika nodded, but could not trust her voice to answer. Nor could she trust her thoughts to avoid what she knew would be happening to Maggie's memory of her if she decided to stay with the

Fairies. Cian's voice forced its way into her mind: *"You will become like a dream barely remembered by that world ... a secret forgotten."*

Joseph had been silent through these words of parting. But he stepped forward and laid his hand gently on Marika's shoulder. "I'll be here to watch out for her, Miss Maggie," he said. Then, looking down at the girl, he revised: "We'll be watching out for each other, I think."

Marika gave Joseph a small, grateful smile. Then she turned to Maggie again. "I've something to give you. Wait here, please," she told her. Marika walked the few yards over to the whitewashed summerhouse that stood subtly in the morning shadows. She disappeared within its recesses for a few seconds. When she reappeared, she had in hand Ishmael. He was clean and well fed, wearing a ragged pair of pants and a fairly new, bright red, hand-knit sweater that fit him just about perfectly. She led him gently to the wagon.

When they reached the wagon, Ishmael's face reflected a quick flit of recognition for his wife and child, but his mind was too far from being healed to do more than that. Caleb jumped from the wagon's bed and threw his arms around the man. Maggie and Joseph stood and watched in joyous silence.

Eventually, Joseph turned toward Marika, but said nothing. Maggie looked briefly at the girl and then at Joseph with expectation. Joseph bent toward Maggie's ear, but it was she who quoted with a wry smile: "Sometimes, it's just best not to ask."

Ishmael was taken into the wagon bed, his wife and baby joined him, as Caleb climbed onto the bench seat and took the reins of the horses in hand. Maggie accepted Joseph's assistance, helping her back onto the bench next to the young boy. Marika walked to the side of the wagon, and stepped up on the wheel. She leaned in and whispered into Ishmael's ear. He looked at her with comprehension, and tears filled his eyes. As they rolled unheeded down his warm brown cheeks, Marika touched the tears on her own face, then placed them on top of his. By this mingling of their tears, both somehow understood they would be forever bound together through a shared grief and search for their individual freedoms. She stepped away, and returned to stand by Joseph's side.

"Goodbye Joseph," Maggie called as Caleb turned the horses to leave the cemetery. "Take good care of each other ... and Doc, too! May God watch over you." Then she craned backwards in her seat, crying out behind them, "I will always remember you, Marika. Always. Decide however you must to be happy – promise!"

"Yes, Miss. I will be doing that. And I will remember you – for as long as I can," Marika replied barely above a whisper.

Joseph was seating himself on the ground next to Danny. He had taken a small coin from his pocket and was placing it carefully on top of the grave. It was a six-pence for luck, he said.

Marika thanked him for it and began to pluck flowering clover to make a chain to leave looped around the headstone as she often did.

"Joseph," she began. "Why are you not going out west with the rest of the Quakers? Why are you staying here? Don't you believe there is a war coming?"

"Yes, I do believe there will be a war. And that's why I'm staying," he answered solemnly. "Folks 'round here will be needing good doctors in a war. This is not a time for me to be running away."

"How soon?" Marika asked.

"Don't know for sure. But within a couple of years, I would think."

"You won't be getting yourself killed now, will you?"

"Hope not. I'll try not to."

"Good."

The friends sat in silence, sharing the peace of the day, as well as the drying of parting tears still fresh in their hearts.

"Joseph," Marika began again. "Will you be walking me back to the forest today, please? Somehow, I just need you to be walking with me a bit."

"Of course, Child. I was going to ask if I could do that very thing," Joseph answered gallantly.

They rose and Joseph gathered the reins of his horse. "Walk or ride?" he invited.

"Walk, please," she replied.

The Decision.

Floating on her back in the middle of the Bay, Marika was counting stars and watching the man in the moon as he peeked from behind a thin cloud. It seemed as if he were winking at her knowingly.

Cian had called her to this swim in the starlight. But now, he was lying by the fire he had built near her above-ground lean-to, which she had reclaimed and moved back into a few days earlier. He was singing – terribly. He had been doing this of late in an attempt to provoke her into blessing the forest with her own music. But, for the moment, she kept him waiting. Waiting until her thoughts and feelings were well touched and examined.

Time had become relevant again. More specifically, hours. "Twenty-six hours from this moment," Marika thought. "My life will be changing forever – however I decide. Twenty-six hours left to share."

The water was fragrant and gentle and cool. Water Babies occasionally tickled her toes or tenderly pulled on a lock of her hair as it trailed across the water like thick streams of fire reflecting the rays of the moon.

Cian reached a particularly unfortunate note that awoke a dozing Conrí and caused him to move yards away from the offending source. Marika could bear it no longer. She began to sing.

Gradually, the Fairies and other night forest creatures came near to immerse themselves in Marika's magic. She came ashore and continued her singing for her friends and hosts of the past year.

When she had finished her mesmerizing serenade, it was deep into the night. Peace lay soft upon them all.

Wee Ann was curled at Marika's feet. She stood and kissed the girl gently on the cheek and whispered: "Choose us, Marika. Stay. But if you go, I will grant you memories of Fairy kisses." It was the longest the small spirit had ever spoken at one time in Marika's presence. And her words both comforted her and tore at her heart.

Fixer then came and took Marika's hand in his. "I hope you stay with us, Marika," he said as he caressed her fingers. "But I know you may choose your own kind … your own kind," he repeated. "If you do, I want you to take with you the ability to find what is lost. You will give great comfort with this gift. Finding is a blessing." He walked quickly back into the forest shadows, his head low.

Nan and Bob poked her on both arms. "One of us wants you to stay, one of us does not," the one on her left said. "So if you don't stay, you'll need to always be able to see both sides of a thing," the one on her right continued. "See both sides, always," they said as they ran away.

One by one, different Fairies came forward and gently touched the girl – stroking her still-damp hair, kissing her cheeks, laying an ethereal hand against her back or shoulder. Each one asked her to stay – but then graciously gave her a unique and wonderful gift to take back to the world of the others if she decided to leave them forever. They truly loved her, so they could let her go, taking with her the best parts of themselves. And they understood the claims of the other world upon her – appreciated the loss she would know if she decided to stay.

Thackeray was one of the last to come up to her. At first, he remained silent, watching his own feet. "Hello, Thackeray," Marika encouraged. "I have appreciated your friendship, your kindnesses," she continued, careful to not use the words *thank you*. But she couldn't go on. Her voice faltered at the mere thought of leaving this enchanted place – never to return or even remember it. How could that be her decision? But how could it not? Thackeray left without a word. His tears conveyed his meaning.

Aisling appeared and sat at Marika's feet. She looked as lovely as the girl could ever remember seeing her. She glowed with a golden light, her face filled with hope and promise.

"Tell me the dream," Marika said.

"The dream is of a new, much-loved daughter among us. A beautiful girl – a magical girl," she chanted. "*You* are the daughter."

Then her form grew dark and forbidding. It was gray and streaked with tears. Alarmed at the sudden change, Marika repeated, but with trepidation: "Tell me the dream."

"This is not a dream," Aisling said lowly.

"Tell me the *vision*," Marika asked.

"Death and cruelty. Black and white. Brothers and sisters against one another. Too much dying. Fire burning. Hate remembered." Her voice trailed into nothingness, along with her form.

Marika shivered and Cian put another log on the campfire.

"And you, Cian? What do you want me to do?" she asked with a sob.

"Decide for yourself, Luv. It's no good if you don't. What I want is for you to be deciding for yourself. To know in your heart it is right and true. That's what it's always been about, hasn't it?" He turned and dove into the Bay in a single fluid motion, barely making a ripple. And Marika was quite alone.

Conrí came to her knee. And somehow she knew that he would

follow her whatever her decision would be. "My forever friend, Conrí," she said as she stroked his ears. "But how can I leave them?" she said to him softly. "How can I ever forget?"

⌘⌘⌘

The morning broke with black clouds and a hidden dawn. The wind was rising. It was warm and wet, the air heavy with threat. Thunder marched across the horizon.

Marika knew she must visit Danny – must go to him before the storm came crashing down upon them.

The trees of the forest were beckoning to her – but to hurry or wait, she could not discern.

She and Conrí reached the cemetery and were gratified that no one else was there. They walked quickly to Danny's grave, no need to hide and crouch behind tombstones and monuments this day.

The trees bent and moaned and creaked in warning. They waved their moss and leaves with mourning howls. Their blossoms broke and blew as scattered tears.

Marika stretched her body across the grave and sang for her brother without any initial greeting. She sang the lullaby she had left with him that day just over a year before – the day Joseph had first taken her to the edge of the forest and the Carolina Bay.

The winds forbade the melody from reaching the heavens. They jealously kept the beauty of it earthbound, well below even the tops of the trees. But her song covered Danny in soft blankets of love.

When she had finished the song, she laid her head against the ground and spoke so low even Conrí could not know the words.

"Danny boy, I'm leaving this world. I'm going to live in the enchanted forest – with the Fairies themselves, Danny – with the magical beings themselves. I don't know if I'll be allowed to remember you – or Joseph or Maggie – or even Da and Gran. I don't know how long I will be able to keep your face before me or in my dreams. But I promise you this, my love – as long as I can hold on to the memories, I will come to you, and bring you proof of my remembering."

She wept a bit, then, but went on: "I will never know you in heaven, Danny – so you must not be waiting for me to come. I will try to remember you here all the more for it. But you and Gran and Da must hold fast to one another – and don't be waiting for me."

A great strike of thunder rolled across their heads. The wind crushed down on them. The sky was white with lightning. Conrí paced and circled the grave urging Marika to come away.

"Goodbye, Danny. Goodbye my darling boy. Forgive me for taking you away from Da and the *thribli* and not keeping you safe and well. Forgive me for holding you unseen and secret. I loved you so much, you see. I just loved you so much."

She kissed the stone as she stood. With great reluctance, she finally, suddenly, turned and ran with Conrí away from Danny and back to the forest. She must tell the Fairies of her decision, she knew. Her heart had become terribly fearful that they would change their minds and not let her stay – not want her after all.

"Hurry, Conrí, hurry!" she pleaded unnecessarily, as they jumped and ran and stumbled their way across the forest floor, nearing the enchanted gates. In her soul she prayed they would be open and waiting for her.

The two reached the magic veil just as the rain began to rush upon them. The wind whipped it from all directions, blurring Marika's vision as it pelted her face unmercifully. She paused to get her bearings and align herself with the gates. Conrí's low growl was lost in the wind and thunder. Then a flash of blinding light illuminated the form of Jacko just in front of them, blocking their way.

"Marika!" was all he shouted above the storm. The long green scarf of sodden silk around his neck whipped wildly in the winds.

"Get away, Jacko," she called with new courage. "Step away, and let us pass."

Instead, he lunged forward and grabbed her arm. She cried out in pain, and Conrí responded in kind – his teeth sinking deeply into Jacko's other arm. The man released the girl immediately, but began kicking and thrusting his heavy boots at the dog.

Marika leapt through the unguarded opening of the veil and grabbed Conrí by the collar to pull him through after her. Conrí, refusing to loosen his grip on the enemy brut, unwittingly allowed Jacko to cross the threshold as well. And behind him, Jacko managed to pull through his horse.

"Leave him," Marika commanded, and Conrí grudgingly relaxed his jaw. Jacko pulled back in pain. Blood flowed from the wound, mixing with torrential water as it coursed down his sleeve.

"Run," Marika again shouted to Conrí, and he responded immediately.

Marika suddenly realized she had no need to call for help from her forest friends. They were already there.

 Cian and Saoirse did not lead her underground this time, however. This time, they steadfastly confronted the evil threatening her. All of the Fairies were, in fact, present in force. A formidable force.

Lightning flashes lit up the faces of devils and hanging bones. Between thunder cracks, the moans and groans of the dead and witches and warlocks called and threatened. Large, drooling bears and fierce, striking snakes loomed. Thick, fat frogs and slithering eels covered the ground.

Jacko pulled his waiting mount into the fray and leapt to its saddle, which offered him the advantages of both height and speed.

Marika ran toward the Bay, but Jacko grabbed at her, sinking his fingers deeply into her long hair.

"Got you, you witch!" he laughed – a sound of pure darkness and evil.

Marika screamed: "You killed my Da! How can you be thinking I could forgive that? I hate you!"

"Did you see me kill him? Or just wearing his scarf? Perhaps I was there – but none can say I did the killing," he responded with great anger.

"You are a liar and a thief," the voice rang out. It came from what looked like Marika standing among the trees. Jacko looked down at his hand still tangled in the hair of the girl he believed was Marika – but as he looked, she changed into a young boy, whom he had never seen before.

"You stole Ishmael and tortured and held him captive," another Marika shouted from behind him.

Jacko turned to stare and reflexively dropped the young boy in his grasp. The child resumed its appearance as Marika.

Jacko swung from one image to the next. "Who are you? Where are you? I've got no quarrel with any but the girl!" he shouted above the storm.

The wind blew a threatening gush, and tree branches whipped at Jacko and his horse.

"Your quarrel is with us all!" the voice pierced the wind – the voice of Saoirse, who stood for freedom of all living beings.

Crack! Whip was there. His lashes competed with the bursts of stunning lightning and wildly swinging branches of trees and torn limbs. The gale continued as the Fairies combated their foe.

Jacko's horse was nearing panic. It reared, but its rider held fast. The man shouted at each Marika that appeared – foul curses and accusations, threats and claims against her, some involving Ishmael and even Danny.

"It was *you* who took him. And it was *you* who brought your Da to harm looking for you. He loved you, and he died for it!" Jacko yelled over the winds.

"No!" Marika ran out in front of the horse in blind outrage.

The frightened animal had withstood all that it could. It reared twice, and then ran as if for its life, regardless of the commands and brutal whipping of its rider. Unable to throw the torture from its back, the wretched horse raced toward the trees – the low-hanging branches. It was successful in its terrorized mission.

Jacko swung in the winds – thrashing, then limp. The long wet length of green silk he had wrapped around his throat was hopelessly tangled in the boughs of a strong, supple pine. The evil was silenced.

At that same moment, the storm exhausted its fury. It left the forest rapidly. Marika was standing beneath the hanging dead man, shaking and stunned. Relief fought with guilt within her belly as well as her soul.

Quietly, quickly, the Fairies surrounded her. Thackeray climbed the tree and made his way to the end of the branch. He cut the dead man free, dropping him into the waiting grasp of the Shifters. None retained the image of Marika now – but took on the appearances of Irish Travellers.

Fixer had found the frightened horse, calmed and comforted him, and was leading him toward them. The Shifters lifted up Jacko's lifeless form and draped it across the back of the animal. Two of them led the tragic burden away and out of the forest. Within the hour, he would be returned to his *thribli*.

As the rain settled into a steady drizzle, and the winds continued to abate, the thunder could be heard only in the distance. The lightning flashed impotently, silently, on the horizon.

Wee Ann and Cian accompanied Marika to the opening of her old underground dwelling. Conrí was already there. With complete ease, the girl and dog both descended to the comfort of the home. Saoirse was waiting to keep them company. Wee Ann fixed tea.

Marika had slept soundly for hours. She awoke to soft whispers. Standing around her were a dozen or more Fairies – all shushing each other to not wake the girl.

"I'm awake," she announced, and the lighting in the apartment came up accordingly.

"It's almost midnight," she was told with meaning. "Come above, come out, pronounce your decision, Child."

Each Fairy disappeared almost immediately, and Marika and Conrí were left alone. "Are we sure, Conrí?" she asked him. He reached out and pulled on her skirt, bringing her closer to the entrance. "Apparently, we are," she laughed. She didn't bother with shoes. For some reason, they seemed unnecessary. She rose to the surface and landed with grace, Conrí at her heels.

All of the gathering was there. Saoirse and Cian remained near to her. As it happened exactly one year before, the Fairies joined hands and called to the spirits of all living things in the enchanted forest. They held time still. The entire woodlands whistled and swirled around them. The air itself turned silver and shimmered and chimed. Cian's eyes glowed and watched Marika closely. Saoise was at her side, but did not touch even her garments. Cian stepped nearer and stood behind Marika. He leaned close and whispered the question into her ear: "You have decided?"

"Yes," she replied.

"And what is your decision?" he asked with his voice of wind.

"I wish to stay here, in the enchanted forest," she said without hesitation. "I ask for both myself and Conrí the dog to be accepted into the gathering of Fairies." Her voice sounded strange in her own ears.

"Do you know the cost?" he challenged softly.

"We well know and accept," Marika responded.

"You will be a part of us forever?"

"We will be a part of you forever and ever."

"Forever," the woods echoed all around them.

"And what say you, Brothers and Sisters?" he called to the rest of the Fairies and forest creatures, without so much as raising his voice above the faint wind-bourn whisper.

"We accept these beings as belonging to us for the rest of always," they responded as one voice.

The forest breathed, as time came alive again. The wind sighed and rushed away to the four corners of the earth.

"Welcome, daughter, sister and friend," Cian pronounced. He laughed with his head thrown far back, and gave three loud claps of his hands. Then he bent to scratch Conrí behind the ears.

The Fairies joined in his laughter, and danced and tightened their circle around the girl and dog.

Immediately, the forest itself took on a different light. The midnight stars were bigger, brighter. The moon's face smiled with shining eyes and a definite wink. The voices of the woods were clear and cheerful. Glorious scents filled the rain-washed air. It was as if a different kind of veil had been lifted, and Marika was now on the right side of it.

Saoirse then placed around Marika's neck her Da's green silk scarf, clean and dry. She tied it carefully and secured it with buttons of acorn tops and ribbons of starlight. She spoke not a word.

Cian kissed away Marika's tears of happiness and said: "Well done, Luv. Welcome home."

The celebration played on until dawn.

Throughout the night, Marika spent much of the time on the edge of the gaiety. Reliving the confrontation with Jacko – re-hearing his words, watching his death – guilt and confusion weighed heavily on her. Then Cian sat himself down beside her. First, he simply watched the revelers. At last he said in an everyday voice: "It was his decision, Luv. Respect it." And then he moved away and went to kick a wayward ball in a rather raucous competition occurring in front of her.

With that, her heart somehow settled. And her thoughts became clear and steady and bright. It was over. Or, perhaps, now it could truly begin.

By morning, the storm itself was done, but the disquieting wind had returned. The trees in the forest bent to its will like tall old men listening to their women's advice. The birds rode its waves, clutching at passing branches. The grasses danced wildly. Flowers scattered their beauty wantonly.

Marika continued to explore and delight in the new enchantments of the forest now revealed to her. Her own mystic powers were intensified as well, and she sat listening to the wind, watching rivers of sunlight, savoring all the enhanced fragrances. She laughed at Conrí as he seemed to be adjusting to and enjoying the same magical transformation.

Since sunrise, her thoughts had been almost entirely for Joseph. She discovered she could focus her wishes even more strongly now, and she called to him to come to the forest.

Near midday – with Conrí at her side – she began to walk toward the gates, the edge of the protected forest, in anticipation of Joseph's arrival. Along the way, both girl and dog continued to rejoice in the uncommon natural beauty and bounty that surrounded them. Marika sang in praise of it all. And the forest quivered – as much from the joy of her music as the winds that whirled and skipped their way through it.

As if from a great distance, Marika at last heard her name being called. Joseph! She almost missed it, so faint it was, so difficult to discern from the wind. Again, the ghost of a call could be heard, saying her name.

She floated through the gates effortlessly. Joseph had his back to her, turning to call in every direction.

"Here I am, Joseph," she said quietly.

He turned to face her with a great smile on his lips. But it slowly melted away.

To his eyes, her image was fading, in and out, light to dark. She appeared as a spirit to him. Her voice was clear, and her face shown with a warm glow. There was a haze about her that the winds of the day didn't stir. From around her neck, a soft green scarf floated out. He knew that scarf.

"Child," he began, but then stopped.

She tried to make it easier for him. "I have made my decision. I am becoming a part of the forest."

"Yes," was all he replied. Then, after a thought, he challenged the words, "Becoming a part of it?"

"Yes, Joseph. It was what I pledged – if I chose this world over the one of the others," she tried to explain.

"You mean, if you chose not to live in the world I belong to," he replied. There was an uncharacteristic touch of bitterness in his voice.

"Yes."

He took a deep breath and looked away as he blinked his eyes and wiped at his nose.

Then he cleared his voice and said, "Then come sit with me Child – for just a bit."

They both moved to the fallen log that had been their shared place of comfort for so many conversations. The site of their Christmas party ... their discussions of slavery and freedom ... her confidences of all her hopes and fears ... all had taken place here. It was a fitting departure point. Marika sat at his side.

"There has been a death in the gypsy camp," he began. "It was Jacko. His *thribli* found his body draped across his horse – after the storm last night."

Marika remained silent.

Joseph continued: "Strangled they say – by his own neck scarf, they think – although *it* is missing." He carefully kept his eyes away from the green silk around Marika's throat.

"Hung," she said, "by his own anger and greed and cruelty. Tangled in a pine branch, he was, by his own horse. It was his own doing, Joseph," she concluded, looking her friend in the eyes with absolute honesty.

"He cannot hurt you now. I'm glad."

She nodded.

"But I am going to lose you, aren't I?" he surmised. There was incredible sadness in his voice. It fairly broke Marika's heart. Her image turned dark and faded almost away. She fought to keep it there, close to him, just a bit longer.

"Please don't go yet," he said alarmed.

"I'm trying not to," she assured him. "It's difficult. But I will be needing to leave you soon, at least leaving your sight of me. I will be able to visit you – but you will have to simply remember me. Please ... remember me, Joseph – for as long as you can. Promise!"

"Yes, Child, of course. I promise you."

She reached for him and held his hand to her tears.

"One more question before you go," he requested with some urgency.

"Yes?" she replied.

"You took Danny from the *thribli*, didn't you – without permission? That was why you couldn't go back. He is the secret you are protecting with your life, isn't he?" He spoke the words, not as questions and without recriminations, but as truths that he had understood for a very long time.

"Yes," was all she said.

The winds lifted the thickness of their silence and broke it into a thousand pieces and scattered them away.

"I will never forget you, Child. I will carry you with me wherever I go, Marika," Joseph said at last.

Even as he spoke, Marika could hear her name being called from behind the enchanted veil. It coaxed and summoned her. She turned and saw vague forms of Saoirse and Cian at the gate. The freedom Fairy walked toward them both. Joseph started and half shut his eyes to her vision.

Saoirse reached out her arms and embraced Marika across her shoulders.

"Come, Child ... it's time to go," she said as she watched Joseph. He recognized his own first words to Marika so long ago. And he realized the girl would be well looked after.

"Cherish and protect her," he said to Saoirse over Marika's head.

"We do," the spirit answered.

Cian reached from the gates and drew Marika back through to him.

"I will remember," Joseph called after them.

"I will remember you, Joseph," her voice floated back to him.

He stood alone. His heart was empty. With a deep sigh of great sadness and resignation, he mounted his horse and turned to ride away.

Then, from all around him, he heard her singing. The wind had calmed to a gentle breeze. The sun grew warm and cleared the sky with a sweep of its rays. The song followed Joseph to the edge of the forest and filled his heart completely with love.

"Will he remember, Cian?" she asked.

"If you wish it. He will remember."

SPRING
1866

The Return.

Joseph arrived at Danny's grave a little before sunset. He had stopped to pray beside the dozen or so achingly new headstones. Rough-cut wood, they were, created as well as could be expected during the thin supplies of a war that had stretched from one year to the next and the next, until half a decade had been spent in men and money and time lost forever. But, finally, it was over. South Carolina was broken in spirit and economy. It would come back, of course. The vanquished always survived somehow, he knew.

He was an old man now. Eleven years had passed since he had first seen the unknown little boy taken from the train in Doc's strong arms. Eleven years and a war and incalculable losses can age a man thoroughly. His shoulders drooped. Perhaps from the countless hours he had spent standing over hard, sad tables tending to men's ravaged bodies. Trying to save limbs and lives. Patching up wounds in boys too young to know such pain. But he and Doc had survived. They had given their best without prejudice. And then, they had resumed a semblance of normalcy in the old house.

He came to visit Danny all through the war, as often as possible. Today, he brought a small tin soldier to put near the headstone. Most of the other gifts had disappeared over the years, although a single carved-tin button still remained.

The sun was soft honey-and-rose colored along the horizon; the old trees were deep black silhouettes against it, with long purple shadows sliding out from their earth-slippered feet. A light breeze picked up the first notes of the birds' twilight song. Tiny white flowers closed their eyes for the night. He savored all the Southern scents released into the air at this magical hour, and treasured all the blessings of this place, which even long years of raging war could not destroy. It gave him peace.

As he approached Danny's grave, he could swear he heard her singing – Marika singing! It was unmistakable. And yet, no one was near. The closer he tried to listen, the fainter it became. His old ears could be playing tricks, he suspected.

His tired eyes blinked and blurred, as he reached the place he sought. There, faint as memories, he could see the imprints of a dog's paws in the soft damp dirt around the grave. A flash of green caught at his eye from the other side of the headstone. Was it a scarf? But upon closer look, equally unexplained, he found a chain of freshly picked and tied flowering clovers draped around the stone.

He rested his small token on top of Danny's grave and spoke to the boy for many long minutes. The singing called to him again then, and he listened, longingly, lost in remembrance.

He touched the earth gently and spoke just above a whisper to the small grave's spirit: "I wonder if the mystery of you will live on after me...the mystery of the unknown little boy who died and was laid to rest here in 1855. Or maybe it will perish from this world along with me." He breathed in deeply and considered the thought: "I must be the only one left now who knows your truth...the truth about the secret child."

THE END

The Celtic symbols used throughout this book were created and are copyrighted by artist Cathey Henley Osborne. Each was developed around specific Celtic folklore and meaning as noted below.

 THE ARRIVAL: **Mouse**
Secrets • Cunning • Shyness

 THE FARM: **Cow**
Contentedness • Defending the inner child • Abundance

 DISCOVERIES: **Badger**
Courage • Tenacity • Dream guidance • Individuality

 SECRETS: **Crane**
Keeping of secrets • Search for truth • Wisdom • Cleverness

 THE DOG: **Hound**
Companionship • Protection • Enduring loyalty

 CHRISTMAS: **Stag**
Independence • Gentleness • Dignity • Endurance • Love

 GOING TO GROUND: **Bear**
Achievement • Instinct • Fortitude • Harmony

 THE TRIAL: **Wolf**
Intelligence • Cunning• Outwitting those who wish you harm

 THE DECISION: **Butterfly**
Fairy faith • Clarity • Freedom

 THE RETURN: **Sparrow**
Remembrance • Memory

About The Author

A professional copywriter for more than three decades, and newspaper columnist since 2004, Marti Healy has received numerous industry writing awards. The majority of her career was spent with a communications firm in Indianapolis, Indiana, where she was vice president and senior writer.

Marti relocated to Aiken, South Carolina, in 2004, where she now shares her home with dogs Sophie and Teddy and cat Sparkey. Since January of 2008, she has devoted her time exclusively to various personal writing projects.

Marti is a popular speaker on the topics of her books as well as her writing career, and enjoys meeting with book clubs and other groups utilizing her books. She has appeared on numerous daytime television shows in the Southeastern area, and has served on panels and as a featured speaker at regional book festivals.

To read more about Marti Healy and her work, or to contact her by email, please visit: MartiHealyBooks.com.

OTHER PUBLISHED BOOKS BY MARTI HEALY:

THE GOD-DOG CONNECTION: *Things I've Learned about God and Faith from the Dogs and Cats in My Life* (The Design Group Press) is a collection of 25 essays that each captures a small vignette of animal behavior, and then the faith lesson that can be drawn from it.

THE RHYTHM OF SELBY: *A gently mysterious novel of the South* (The Design Group Press) is set in the fictitious town of Selby, South Carolina. This was Marti's first novel, and was the recipient of the **Independent Book Publishers Bronze Medal for excellence in the Popular Fiction category in 2009**.